FROM WARRIORS TO WARRIOR WRITERS

JOURNEYS TO HEALING

Edited by
Sara Hollcroft
with Erika K. Hamilton

HUMANITIES NEBRASKA

NEBRASKA WRITING PROJECT

DISCLAIMER:

Any views, findings, conclusions, or recommendations expressed in this book do not necessarily reflect the views of Humanities Nebraska, Nebraska Cultural Endowment, National Endowment for the Humanities, Nebraska Writing Project, or Nebraska Warrior Writers.

ISBNs   978-1-7360023-0-8 (paperback edition)
         978-1-7360023-1-5 (eBook edition)

BISACs:
FIC000000   FICTION/General
POE000000   POETRY / General
BIO008000   BIOGRAPHY & AUTOBIOGRAPHY / Military

Cover & interior design by Ryan Simanek

Printed in the United States of America for

HUMANITIES NEBRASKA

Lincoln, Nebraska

FROM WARRIORS
TO
WARRIOR WRITERS

JOURNEYS TO HEALING

CONTENTS

IN THE BEGINNING...

"Interested in giving input into a new writing group for veterans? Humanities Nebraska has this idea..."

In November 2013, Executive Director Chris Sommerich and Dr. Erika Hamilton represented Humanities Nebraska, a non-profit organization, at the National Humanities Conference in Birmingham, Alabama, where they learned about Missouri Humanities' writing workshops for veterans and their annual anthologies. As Sommerich and Hamilton sat in the Birmingham airport, waiting for their flight home, they decided to call Dr. Robert Brooke, Director of the Nebraska Writing Project and Professor of English at the University of Nebraska-Lincoln, to see if a similar program could begin in Nebraska.

Several meetings took place in the spring of 2014 to sketch out a vision of what it could look and feel like. Beverly Hoistad came in as support from the Nebraska Writing Project. The NWP had experience with families in reading-based activities. They had experience both with teaching and with teachers at all levels in further development and research about writing. They also had a great bank of teachers experienced at working with different levels and ages of writers. They pulled in a few veterans, one being Ron Carter, to get opinions and advice on the startup. Later, Scott Gealy and Hoistad met twice with psychologists working at the VA Hospital in Lincoln, Nebraska. They met to prepare for what they might hear and to receive advice on "trigger" words/situations. The doctors were very supportive in preparing Gealy and Hoistad for future conversations, readings, and responses to their writers, and one of them always attended the first series of six writing workshops during the Fall of 2014, creating a support net for the veterans.

Lori Wardlow worked behind the scenes at the VA Hospital, providing inspiring room space in the VA auditorium, "booking" their dates and room, and letting the security guard know. She put the word out, posting vivid posters for the group in Lincoln. SheriLynne Hansen of Humanities Nebraska also made posters for the Omaha and Grand Island/York meetings for veterans. Hoistad called every VFW Post in Lincoln and visited all the public libraries to post Wardlow's and Hansen's posters and flyers. She also started lining up "outside" speakers, knowing they would add more speakers when they discovered better where the writers' interests lay.

It took just one planning meeting to hook Hoistad into this new writing class of veterans. She knew she wanted to be a part of it. It was her honor and privilege to help the men and women get their stories down, see them grow as writers and be a part of a writing community.

By day, she was a primary teacher and Gealy, also a Teacher Consultant with the Nebraska Writing Project, was a high school teacher. On Saturdays, they would be facilitators to adult students (they viewed them as the super heroes wearing the capes). Hoistad and Gealy met several times to discuss what it would look like and to divide teaching responsibilities. The classes would be two hours long on Saturday mornings, 9-11 with enough time, if needed, to run over until the VA closed at noon. Both teachers felt Saturdays would be when they were fresh and also easier for those veterans with a 40-hour work week. The Nebraska Writing Project had long-running success with its research, teachers teaching teachers, speakers, presentation of information with active learning, small inti- mate reading, writing, and response groups, and occasional large group sharing of writing "celebrations." Free "stuff," time to socialize, and major "snackage" also worked for both groups. They would proceed forward accordingly.

Hoistad and Gealy met more than an hour early that first Saturday morning, as excited as they were each year for the start of school and the new adventure. They arranged all the "freebies"—pencils, pens, spiral notebooks, binders, plastic slip covers, post-its, highlighters. The two-seater tables were arranged in a circle, and the home-made refreshments and juice on a covered table waited for the writers at the back of the room. Hoistad was determined to make the money go as far as possible, so she used coupons, school sales at stores, and personally made the treats in order to have enough money left over to continue in the spring. She states, "I just didn't want to poison anyone—I was careful." Hoistad and Gealy made perfect partners. They had books to read and discuss writing choices: Art Speilman's Maus and Weisenthal's The Sunflower. Each participant received a copy of <u>Maus</u> to keep. <u>The Sunflower</u> book was borrowed (with permission) from a local high school.

The doors opened on a September Saturday in 2014. It was an even mix of men and women that first day and continues so. The first year the numbers were low, but steady. Some came for a few meetings, others for the season. Many have stayed in contact as their schedules shift and either have joined again in Lincoln or in Omaha with leaders, Jen Stastny and Cindy Cronn. There was a vet writing group in Grand Island with dedicated writers as some of them had to drive an hour or more each Saturday just to get to the writing session and another hour or more to drive home. Grand Island's group was led by facilitators Judy Lorenzen, Karrie Wiarda, Danielle Helzer, Erin DeHart, and Mark Houston. Unfortunately, this ended when their leaders were not able to continue and there was no one else available to step in.

At the end of Lincoln's first six workshops, Hoistad and Gealy were afraid if they ended in early October, the writers would lose interest and not be back in January or February for the start of the next session. They agreed to create extra sessions to keep their writing group together as they had bonded, and the stories were growing deeper in content. Besides, they just didn't want to stop. So they met twice a month until the sessions started again in January. This tradition continues with a Lincoln group meeting an hour (or more) every week to write and respond to others' writings. For the Omaha group, they add a marathon at the end of their spring and fall sessions.

Beverly Hoistad and Scott Gealy paved the way for the current Lincoln leaders, Sara Hollcroft and Tom Seib, and the Omaha leaders, Jen Stastny and Cindy Cronn, to continue the success of the Nebraska Warrior Writers' groups. Years go by and new writers show up. The "new" leaders still have presentations on author's notes, generating ideas, revision, developing characters, style, voice, publishing and the list goes on, sparking new insights to the writers as their writing expands but also giving new members the knowledge to grow as writers. Writing marathons, coffeehouses, and the Spring Gathering in May continue.

The veterans have been written about in the *Humanities Nebraska* Rapport Magazine (Issue 6/Winter 2014) and NET Nebraska visited the VA to do a seven-minute piece that resulted in a story for "Nebraska Stories" shown on PBS Thursday nights. Another article was published in Issue 21/Winter 2019 about the Nebraska Center for the Book's Jane Geske Award being given to the Nebraska Warrior Writers group, recognizing their contribution to literacy.

Hoistad said, "These writing veterans deserve every accolade and celebration for their writing."

The current leaders, the veteran writers, and the readers want to thank the Nebraska Writing Project, Robert Brooke, and Humanities Nebraska for all of their support throughout the years. A special thanks goes to the foresight and leadership of Beverly Hoistad and Scott Gealy.

Editor's note: The submissions and editing for the anthology is taking place during the Covid 19 Pandemic. As I type this, there is controversy over when it will end. Lives have been changed and lives have been lost. That hasn't stopped us from writing. We write to achieve a goal, to have or make an impact, or we write to overcome what life throws at us.

WARRIOR WRITERS

On a crisp Saturday autumn morning, several men and women entered the Veteran Administration office in Lincoln, Nebraska. Their counterparts in Omaha and Grand Island/Kearney area were also gathering at their meeting places. Since 2014, they have met six weeks in the fall and again in the spring. Now, due to the coronavirus outbreak, the groups have joined together in zooming their Saturdays' sessions. The groups include Vets, active military, and family members of Vets, and they are called the Warrior Writers.

Several are Viet Nam Vets who find a safe harbor for writing with other vets. Or as a Veteran from Desert Storm states, "A knowledge that we are not alone." They want to write. "We all wore the uniform of our country, and we accept each other unconditionally." One of the original members of the Warrior Writers, states he was not a writer before attending the writing group, but now he is. Another Vet likes the safe place to share her writing and her heart with Veterans who understand what she has been through in her career. She states, "They have become her friends who push her to be a better person."

Another female writer writes about her sexual assault while in the military. Another is outlining a book on her own assault, ready to name names. For them, writing helps liberate them from their past shadows. Perhaps then, they can retake control. Perhaps then, sleep comes easier. Perhaps then, the powers-to-be will listen. Warrior Writers through the support of the Nebraska Writing Project and Humanities Nebraska give these vets support and hope.

Warrior Writers do not write about their experiences of combat, but some write about their attempt to heal afterwards. The poem "The Healing Wall" by Andy Gueck speaks of family and friends who visit the wall for hope when the name they seek is not there or closure when it is. However, it might be said that the wall is not for the soldier, but for the person who spit on the soldiers, who called them worthless and baby killers. It is those people who need to heal, to learn to forgive themselves.

The Warrior Writers' program helps Vets heal through the sharing and acceptance of their writing with other Vets. They laugh together hearing a story about grilling meat on a car's engine as a fellow Vet's family drives the long miles to their destination. Laughter heals. And, they understand the sorrow of death of other Vet's family member. There is a sense of knowing without actual knowing when a fellow Vet needs comforting, who is struggling with life itself. They have been there themselves. Warrior Writers helps Vets be heard, accepted, appreciated, and valued.

A Vet who is a novelist in the making, shared that the Saturday sessions help him to hone in on his writing skills without outside pressure. Guest speakers, books on the craft of writing, revision, publishing, all paid by Humanities Nebraska working with Warrior Writers help members to improve and expand their writing. Writers learn to recognize and trust their growth as writers. It often tells them something they didn't know about themselves—that they are stronger than they thought. Writing empowers them. Writing is a way to shine a beacon of light for others. It can be an act of defiance, but for most of the writers, it is a labor of love, faith, and hope.

As to the name of the writing group, in the words of Joel Elwell and Andy Gueck (two of the Lincoln based group), "The title, 'Warrior Writers,' describes who we were, not who we are." And so, the warriors write on.

For more information about Nebraska Warrior Writers, contact Humanities Nebraska or visit NEwarriorWriters.org.

ACKNOWLEDGMENTS

To our Warrior Writer Group facilitators

From Mary Baker, Andy Gueck, Sharon Robino-West, three of the first Nebraska Warrior Writers

Writing prompt: What do the Warrior Writer facilitators mean to you?

Thank you for being a friend
You get us going
Provide writing prompts
Facilitate our learning about writing, about ourselves, about the writing industry
You edit our work
You share our struggles and our victories
You've supported us as friends could, helped us as teachers would, loved us as a family should.

Thank you to the Warrior Writer Facilitators:

It takes a special person to give of their personal time, energy, and Saturday mornings to facilitate a writing workshop for military veterans. Our facilitators are teachers by profession, so they are trained for the job, but the training is not what makes the difference. The Warrior Writer facilitators truly care about the veterans who have attend these workshops over the past five years.

These teachers are writers too, and they are passionate about writing and guiding others along their writing journey. They are not here by accident; they are drawn to the program by their love for writing and their personal connection to those who have served our country in the armed forces. While they may not be veterans themselves, they have ties to veterans, and they know how important it is for the veteran's stories to be told, written and come to life.

From the first teachers, Bev Hoistad and Scott Gealy, to Tom Seib, Sara Hollcroft in Lincoln, and Darin Jensen to the current Omaha facilitators Jen Stastny, and Cindy Cronn, and Judy Lorenzen, Karrie Wiarda, and Danielle Helzer from Grand Island, all have a keen passion for encouraging the words and the stories that need to be told. They help pull them out of us as veterans, warriors, and survivors. This group is a family, a brotherhood and sisterhood, a tribe, our tribe, and a meaningful part of our world. As veterans we are not easily won over. You must earn our trust. We are trained to be tough, so we may not like criticism or feedback. We tend to be bull-headed and stoic, and are likely to speak bluntly with no filters, but that does not faze our facilitators. They put up with us like they do any of their students and press us close to their hearts while providing encouragement along the way.

In addition to our Warrior Writer facilitators, we have been blessed to have many guest speakers over the years. These guests have been writers and teachers who have come and inspired us throughout the sessions, and have become our friends as well. Our sessions have been graced by Poet Laureates, authors, university professors and other passionate poets and writers.

We are deeply grateful for our facilitators and guest speakers, as they have stuck with us over the past few years and helped us build a wonderful Warrior Writers Program. Your guidance, encouragement and facilitation have created an environment where our writing can flourish, and we can grow as writers. A special thank you to Humanities Nebraska as well, for sponsoring these workshops for veterans and believing in the importance of a program that reaches military veterans. So thank you all for your time and sacrifices and spending your time as part of our tribe! We look forward to many more years together.

WORKSHOPPING DURING THE "TIME OF CORONA"

Editor's note: The following dialogue was recorded by Sharon Robino-West on May 9, 2020, during the Warrior Writers' first Zoom session during the Covid 19 pandemic. They have gotten much better since then.

"Hello…"

"Can anybody see me?"

"Is my audio on?"

"I see you. Turn your volume up."

"Wait—Cindy is texting me…
She can't get in on the password we're using."

"Okay, I'll see if I can get her in here."

"I like your background!"

"Jack, can you play us a song? I see all those guitars on your wall."

(From Jen's cell phone) "Cindy, if you can hear me…Oh, I see you on the screen now."

"Hey everyone, the password has changed. Zoom in its wisdom just changed it. Here comes the new one."

"Good to see you all. I think we're all in the room now."

"Now that you're all here, next we're going to go into break-out rooms. We've got this!"

(A collective sigh rises, along with mumbling…)

ODE TO 2020
by Sharon Robino-West

It's the little things
that carry me through--
they always do.
I learned once upon a time on Parris Island
on graduation morning
blue jeans
drive-through hamburgers
the scent of seawater drifting in the wind
faith and family,
these were not little things
instead
they are important things.

It's the sheer scale of things
the overwhelming weight of heaviness
somber and suffocating
the angst in not saying goodbye
and not saying hello
at the moments when life ends and begins again.

I miss people
miss parks
miss haircuts

and the freedom to come and go.
It's the depth of joy in these small moments
that carries me through
and they will carry me through this
too.

It's the breadth and the magnitude
of our overwhelming gratitude
to nurses and doctors,
sanitation workers,
teenagers at the grocery
behind the plexiglass
volunteers making face masks
when there aren't any to be found
in this spring of sadness and
dis-ease.

SAYING GOODBYE

by John Achor

The cold penetrated everything as the humid air of an Indiana winter can. It was mid-January 1941 and the seven-year old boy shivered in the dark parking lot of the National Guard Armory in Indianapolis. His mother placed a comforting hand on his shoulder.

The engines of huge U. S. Army trucks grumbled into life and belched thick exhaust fumes. Headlights penetrated the darkness. Engines idled while men in uniform shouted orders to others and supervised the loading of the trucks. Equipment, already onboard, awaited the troops who would be traveling south to Camp Shelby near Hattiesburg, Mississippi. The boy strained to stand on tiptoe hoping for a glimpse of his father.

Hours ago at home, his dad explained what would happen this evening. "I'll be very busy tonight, so I may not be able to talk to you. I may not even see you in the crowd. I hope so, but maybe not." The boy nodded but didn't comprehend the explanation.

He looked at the sleeve of his father's uniform shirt. The outlines of the patches were still visible. He knew they were marks of military rank. "Where did your sergeant stripes go?" he said.

"Since we are expanding to a full division, my position calls for a higher rank. I've been promoted," his father said pointing to the two silver bars on each collar. "Let's put some of these toys back under the Christmas tree, so you can play with them later."

The boy reveled in the attention his father was showing him and enjoyed the time they spent together on the living room floor.

His father continued, "I want you to know I love you and I will be thinking about you all the time I am gone. While we're alone here, I'll say goodbye now." He leaned forward and kissed his son on the cheek.

The boy shivered in the dark again. All the time I'm gone, he thought. What did it mean? He was not very close to his father, but he was used to him coming home every night. And now ... Gone — where? How long? He heard the word "war" in whispered conversations between his mother and father. War. He knew the word, but struggled with a full understanding of the concept. He was aware people in wars sometimes died. But ... how did they die? How many? Which ones?

He was used to his father coming home each night — what if his father was one who would die in the war. A shiver wracked his body and he knew it was not from the cold.

His mother felt his body quiver and turned up the collar on his jacket. She knelt in front of him and adjusted the aviator cap and tugged the flaps down snug over his ears. "It won't be much longer," she said. "I think the trucks will be leaving soon. When we get home, I'll make you some hot Ovaltine. That will be good, won't it?"

The boy pulled the ear flaps back up — for two reasons. Only the *dumb* kids wore the flaps down, and the cold wasn't causing him to shiver. He looked for his father and wished with all his might it would not be the last time he ever saw him.

Pushing between some of the adults, he got a better view of the controlled chaos around the trucks. He saw a man break out of the sea of uniforms and start toward him. It was his father — his father was coming over to see him. Someone behind the man shouted, "Captain." His father stopped, turned around and disappeared back into the ocean of humanity.

His mother took him by the hand and they moved to another location — one nearer the exit gate of the assembly area. They watched and waited. At long last, the first truck bucked into motion and steered for the gate. One-by-one the other vehicles moved forward and fell in behind one another forming a long single line. The trucks reminded him of elephants he saw in a circus parade his father took him to see. He smiled.

The boy stretched to see as each of the trucks passed his vantage point. Not seeing his father, he shook his head at each truck then concentrated on the next. The last truck went through the gate, and he never saw his father.

He thought of the words: death, gone, war ... the shiver wracked his body again. His mother hugged him near to her and started for their car saying, "Let's go home."

Home. The boy thoughts turned to the hot chocolate drink his mother promised earlier. He was at peace and the images of a dead soldier melted away like the tail lights on the last truck disappearing into the darkness.

The End

The bustle in a house
The morning after death
Is solemnest of industries
Enacted upon earth –
The sweeping up the heart
And putting love away
We shall not want to use again
Until eternity –
(Emily Dickinson)

HANKIES

by Sara Hollcroft

It was the week after Memorial Day, 2017, that she decided it was time to clean out the box under the counter in the laundry room. Oh, she had piddled around in the past cleaning around it, but had yet to pull it out and fully investigate its contents again. Perhaps it was the visit to her parents' graves the previous week that dispelled some of her feelings of daughter inadequacies and a reoccurring dream of cherries on a branch that led her to take on this particular chore. Perhaps. Or perhaps she was ready for the tears she knew she needed and didn't care if she couldn't control them.

Suppressed memories of her mother had kept her awake for the last two nights. A mother who fought for her daughter to attend college when there was no money. A mother who fought the tough battle of breast cancer and won only to lose the battle of respiratory ailments several years later. And in between those battles was the fight her mother refused to take on. The decision to lose contact with a close family member who had molested her daughter. It was in this battle that the daughter walked away from her mother and never traveled the path home again.

Due to the passage of time, the box, duct taped shut, was relatively easy to open or perhaps it was as if its inhabitants, too, were ready to be free. There was a yellowed, faded newspaper dated Saturday, August 1, 1981, protecting the box's contents from dust. Its headlines were of South Africa: Cape Town trying to oust hundreds of homeless blacks. The paper was placed there, not necessarily to remember Cape Town and its homeless, but to acknowledge that homelessness was a global thing, and because August 1st just happened to be her birthday. She carefully set the newspapers aside not wanting to remember why she had purposely chosen that particular paper to use as a cover inside the box.

Under the first layer of doilies that her mother had carefully and lovingly embroidered were the handkerchiefs she was seeking. There were 22 of them in all. Roses in all colors but especially in red dominated the collection. Her mother's favorite color and favorite flower. But the one hanky she remembered the most was missing. Red cherries on brownish branches. The last time she saw it was the day she and her mother agreed to disagree. It is interesting that nothing else stuck with her, not the actual words that were spoken, nor the meal they had shared. Just that her mother's hanky was partially visible from under the strap of her bra, peeking out from the sleeveless blouse onto her bare shoulder. For some reason, this was the hanky she needed to hold right now, after all these years.

Digging deeper, there, folded in between two other hankies, she found her mother's favorite. Red cherries on brownish branches. It was slightly larger than the palm of her left hand as she unfolded it and placed it there. The tips of her right hand gently caressed the cherries. It was as she remembered, only thinner. Then she looked at the two hankies that had protected it. They, too, were paper thin from usage and age. They weren't as familiar to her, at least to her memory of what her mother had carried with her daily. One was plain, just white with some yellowing. Its four corners were of cotton lace. A vague memory of it was what her mother had called her "going to church" hanky. It never made it to the bra strap as that would have been unchristian, but the patent leather black purse her mother held in church carried it well.

The other one was of a cross outlined in blue in the upper right hand corner of the material. In the lower left hand corner were sunflowers tilted right toward the cross. One flower in the lower right hand corner was a single sunflower with its petals facing upward to the cross. No memory of the hanky existed for this one. Her mother hated sunflowers, and she hated any commercial religious display. This hanky must not be hers, and yet here it was. And, it obviously had a special connection to the cherry branch hanky as it had protected it in its folding.

She pulled up a stool and sat down staring at the open box. She desperately wanted a glass of wine right now. How much of her memory of her mother's likes and dislikes were accurate? Her mother's path had stayed its course those past years. In and out of hospitals were the norm. She had visited her mother during her stay, but only when she was sleeping. Deciding what to talk about kept her from trying. Did the nurses tell her that her daughter had been there?

All of this became moot when the doctors intubated her mother to keep her alive, but also making her a living "vegetable." After much hesitation and agreement that her mother would not want to "live" like that, the family's decision to "pull the plug" was made. A collective gasp went out when they were told that goodbyes needed to be said now since she would only live 5-10 minutes after being taken off life support.

Eight hours later, her mother was still hanging on. While she did not respond to the family, she was still with them. Her sister-in-law and she spent the time with her, talking to each other and often leaning over the bed to include her in the conversation. About dinner time, they without even discussing it, leaned in and whispered in her ear, "It's okay. We will be okay." At first, there was no response and then to their surprise she gracefully, raised her body from the waist up with her right arm raised toward the ceiling. Her frail thin body from the waist down was still parallel to the bed, but her upper torso was at at 45degree angle from the bed. It could not have been comfortable and seemed impossible for such a frail woman. And yet, there she was. The two watchers asked her what she was seeing. There was no response and yet her position stayed the same with her arm extended towards the ceiling. It was obvious that she was seeing something that the other two were not. They both put their hands on her arm and pushed down, but the arm did not waiver as it continued to reach upward toward some invisible sight or thing.

It was at this time a nurse came in and gave her mother a shot of morphine. Almost instantly, her arm came down. Her body relaxed back onto the mattress. Her bowels were released. Her final breath was taken.

All of things she had wanted to tell her mother were now impossible. Regret turning into tears swelled like a dam in a heavy rain as she approached the bed and kissed her mother's forehead goodbye. A flashback of tears years ago cut into the silence turning into anger then dissipated into a deeper sense of loss. With her mother gone, there was no longer a path back home to be found.

Now, 36 years later, she caressed the unfamiliar hanky's cross, and lovingly folded it back as she had found it. Then she gently pushed it under her left bra strap, leaving the cross to cover her heart. A quietness enveloped her, and as she bowed her head, she finally talked to her mother.

OVER THE HINDU KUSH
by Jack Pryor

The Hindu Kush spread below like rocky fingers, grasping the tectonic plates over which it stretched. A million lives carried on within its valleys, so isolated they had never seen a foreigner. Some of them bore little clue their nation, Afghanistan, fought alongside the United States of America, and they cared not a whit. They and their kin had already outlasted the Russians, then the warlords, and then the Taliban. They would still be here, even if a reborn Kublai Khan rode over the ridge with his mounted archers. They would till the rocky soil, plant the poppy, and gather water from the streams which ran off the Hindu Kush's snow pack.

Regardless, Americans lingered up in the sky while across numerous valleys more Americans positioned themselves in makeshift forts built from gravel and sand. They huddled around barren tables to play Halo or call on Skype back home. They went on patrols and tried communicating to the locals – to win "hearts and minds," per the latest general appointed to solve the war and to remind Americans back home it still existed.

This general was different, or so it was promised by this particular president. This general had been in special operations. He ran nine miles every morning, starting at 0500. He would turn Afghanistan around. Then like his predecessor, he ordered the Marines to take the village called Marjah. The Taliban were back, poppy was growing, the locals were being intimidated and shaken down, and the Afghan police were taking bribes.

Hanging in the air, in a continuous figure eight, lingered a black and gray jet called the RC-135. It served to aid the Marines attempting to retake Marjah again. The RC-135 is a reverse engineered from a Boeing 707. B-707's have not been used in civilian flight since the early 1980s. A B-707 had been John F. Kennedy's Air Force One. The RC-135 roared its turbofan engines over the uncaring Hindu Kush and its resilient people. Packed with sensors and people, its job was to listen. Its call sign was "Vacuum," sucking up everything it could detect. Aboard the plane, the crew took naps, made chicken nuggets and pizza, or stared at their screens in between anticipation and catatonia. Among the crew was the single airman aboard trained to halfway know one of the languages those people in the valleys actually spoke.

The aircraft smelled like burnt popcorn, metal, and wires. The engine roar bellowed inside the steel fuselage. Everyone stank. They sweated themselves half to death on the tarmac, the plane reaching 123 °F inside until takeoff, when the HVAC systems kicked on and dropped the internal temperatures fifty-eight degrees. Then their sweat chilled them and they clutched onto blankets. A couple of airmen slipped on winter weight jackets.

Aft of the mission crew, a pungent smell emerged. People perked up but it was just more popcorn. Information flashed onto screens laid before each crew position. That one airman, who had been hastily trained for this area, thought he had found something. The manager and an analyst queried him, he futzed for details, and then they wrote a report and sent it out. This data would "protect the guys on the ground," the manager said. The airman had more to scan, most of it idiomatic town speak for which no military school could prepare.

The people down below in the Hindu Kush and surrounding deserts lived complex lives. They spoke multiple dialects and languages, switching in mid-conversation like nothing, maybe spitting out a few words the linguist recognized from his textbooks. He tried parsing together something, anything. The nation was counting on him to do this, yet he typed while wondering if his efforts mattered. He pictured writing nonsense on slips of paper, tossing them out of the airplane, and getting a medal for it. The manager, the airman realized, would report success regardless of what happened. The only metrics tracked anyway were the take-off, on-watch, and landing times.

An acrid stench broke his concentration. It spewed and spread through the jet. The smell overpowered the RC-135's baked-in odors. People coughed. The manager ordered everyone onto oxygen. He called on the plane's intercom to report a possible fire. The maintenance crew, acting as firefighters, sprang out of their stupor. They shut down equipment and rack after rack powered down. The roaring lessened. One could hear the maintainers' hectic back and forth. The pilot ordered the crew back to base. The mammoth steel can whipped out of its orbit and back towards Pakistan. After the crew strapped in and slipped on their oxygen masks, they noticed their masks sticking to their faces. Everyone one flexed in and out with their breaths. The plane's supplemental oxygen had leaked out. The pilot goosed the throttle. The smoky stench faded while each crew member felt and smelled rubber against their faces.

Meanwhile, the Taliban launched rocket grenades onto some of the Americans. The Marines returned fire to pin down unseen foes. A Predator UAV, swooping above, found young, barely literate men on a ridge. The kill chain started: a Marine lieutenant acknowledged a sergeant's demand for close air support. The Predator locked on and fired its Hellfire missiles. Rocks and debris erupted. The Marines chased the Taliban off. Marjah changed hands again, but only for a short while.

In a village a few miles and a world away, children gathered water, women kept cooking fires going, and men drank tea. The RC-135 returned to base. Another jet prepared to launch. The Hindu Kush darkened in the dusk, home fires and flaming rubble lighting up its shadowed valleys.

THE RAT

by Andy Gueck

One evening as I was returning to my billet from another part of the base, I walked past the A Company Alert Barracks. Suddenly, I could hear a commotion inside, far beyond the normal roar. I wondered if I wanted to see what was going on? Or, if I should call the 1SG, or just ignore it and go drink beer? Did I really need to get involved with this shit?

I walked to the door, opened it and stepped inside. The barracks held about 20 troops and all were at one end of the room, being held hostage by a rat. Now those of you who have never seen a southeast Asian rat, they are about 6-8 inches tall at the shoulder and could walk through a building calling, "Here kitty, kitty."

Upon seeing the mess inside, I asked, "Who is in charge?"

A young soldier responded from the scrum with, "I believe I am, Sargent."

"What the hell is going on in here?"

"Well SGT, PFC Holmes' mother sent him a pellet gun from home, and he thought he could kill this rat that has invaded our billet."

"What kind of stupid is occupying these quarters? A pellet gun is not going to do any more than just piss off your rat if you do hit and wound it, and now you all are facing the consequences."

Now, I was armed with my normal on base weapon, a M1911, .45 caliber pistol. A standard issue weapon for some members of the US Military. Much easier to carry than an M16 rifle. I moved so there was nothing beyond the rat but an empty wall and removed my pistol from its holster and shot the rat. Upon impact, there were bits and pieces of rat scattered over most of the billet. I holstered my weapon, turned and walked out of the billet area and immediately entered the A Company Orderly Room (Where the Commander and the 1ST had their offices). I told the young soldier on duty to contact the Staff Duty Officer, the 1SG, and the Commander and inform them that a weapon was discharged in the Company area. Then follow their instructions.

Within 10 minutes, the Orderly room and immediate area was inundated with people wanting to know what was going on. The Military Police even showed up to check on the report of a weapons discharge. Finally, the Commander, 1SG, Staff Duty Officer and myself were in the Commander's office and I was explaining again what had happened and why I had discharged a weapon on base.

I looked the CO directly in the eye. "Captain, if I had not done something, you probably would have been missing part if not all of your reaction force due to wounds incurred from assault by rat."

The 1SG was struggling to keep a straight face and the CO just broke into laughter. He responded, "SGT Gueck, thank you for rescuing my troops, but next time please find a better means than shooting. They will be up all night cleaning the rat parts out of their barracks."

"Yes, Sir. I will do my best, Sir."

At this point, the Staff Duty informed me that I was expected in his office at 0800 Hours the next day do see the Post Commander.

"Yes, Sir, I will be there. Am I dismissed?"

The 1SG looked and me and said," Gueck, get the hell out of here and drink a beer for me."

"Will do, Top."

The next morning, I was waiting for 0800 hours when my immediate Commander and the Post Commander arrived and after saluting them, was told to follow them into the Colonel's office. The Command Sargent Major brought coffee for everyone, and we were all told to be seated. The Colonel looked at me and shaking his head, "Gueck, you do not look like a rat murderer, but according to my A Company Commander and my Staff Duty, you most certainly are. What do you have to say for yourself."

"Sir, I was just trying to restore order and save the lives of those idiot troops."

At that point, the entire office was overwhelmed with laughter. The Colonel looked at my commander and said, "Major, he is one of yours, deal with him, but I think it was well done; Sgt Major, your opinion?"

"Sir, the look on those troops this AM was priceless. All night they were cleaning and hoping that they got it all, and the young man who formerly owned the pellet gun was being ignored by everyone. I think it is handled, Sir."

"Gueck, get out of my office and try to restrain your urge to shoot rats in the future."

"Yes, Sir."

And, as the saying goes, "No Good Deed Ever Goes Unpunished."

MERMAID'S CASTLE

by John Petelle

I spent three years before the mast,
an apprentice seaman
under French colors
flown in honor of His Majesty,
King Charles IX.

My ship was under sail
three weeks past Madagascar.
Two wicked days of storms,
two wind-lashed nights,
undid us.

Ripped the canvas, split the hull
of our spirited wooden lady,
Bijou de Danse,
broken by Poseidon's trident.

I saw Captain Delacroix,
lashed to the wheel
with ropes, desperate to save her
even past the end.

Nine of the crew fought free,
eight brave souls and I,
clinging to timbers,
as the ocean roared.

When the waves calmed,
peaches and cream were ladled
over the horizon.
The sharks came.

Each man's screams were brief.
Barely echoing,
as my comrades vanished,
until I alone remained.

How I wished the waiting to end.
I ducked my head below,
seeking to spare myself,
flee the pain,

but each time,
I rose gasping,
my body unwilling to concede
to mind's desire.

At last, the touch came,
Soft at my ankle
nudging upward,
as if
caressing my leg
before taking it.

When the water breached beside me,
there were no razored teeth,
no dead black eyes,
only beauty beyond angels.

Auburn hair shining,
swirling between us,
teasing the sight
of her pale skin.

Then she smiled,
lips of coral over pale pearls,
a glimpse of pink tongue
as she laughed, dove beneath me,

graceful fins leaping towards the sky,
iridescent tail twinkling
emerald and sapphire
in the early light.

Scent of fresh kelp
riding the breeze,
brined with life,
perfume of the sea.

Then her hands holding my arms,
her merry eyes diving into mine
as she leaned backwards
and I felt her swimming us.

Faster than dolphins, we surged,
her bare torso breaking the waves,
a spray of drops on my face
as she rescued me.

Rescued, I stay still,
for the sharks never touched me.
Though I am her trophy,
sure as a prize in a fisher's net.

It was not a home we journey to,
more an island display case,
far from land.
No soil or trees.

A basking spot, I think now,
where she revels in the sun,
the open air.
Where she treasures both worlds.

Here she brought me, and here I stay.
Touched by her immortality, I think.
By my daily tallies, sixty-three years.
Yet I remain the youth who sailed.

This outcropping,
scarce the size of the quarter deck,
nineteen stairs from lower landing
to the upper crest.

She tends me well,
fresh fish, shelled mussels,
even mystery fruit
from the sandy deeps.

Her pet, in all manner of ways.
Each month, at the fullest moon,
she walks on human feet,
skin-clad legs, climbing steps to me.

Our kisses taste of salt,
of Neptune's kitchen.
For three nights, she remains changed,
then departs.

She may have kinfolk I have never seen,
or she may wander her marine currents alone.
I,
her sole possession.

Speculation is all I own here,
in this remote eternity.
If I am imprisoned,
I no longer want to leave.
In the evening sky,
the goddess of tides grows full.
I await my rescuer, at peace.
I am forever claimed.

DON'T CAGE THIS HEART

by Cynthia Douglas-Ybarra

I would not cage this heart, cutting off life giving blood
Coursing through chamber and valve,
Keeping time with the universe.
The tick tock, lub dub more than machinations
And electrical impulse moving the muscle inside
This chest.

The heart is the keeper of secrets,
The gauge of passion,
The temple of lovers.
It guides vulnerable body toward the other
Opening up, gentle hands, soft lips
Sweet caresses.

I would not harden this heart
Against the free flight of love
Even when fear sits on sternum,
Stopping breath, searing pain through body and soul.
This heart is more than the sum of its parts
Chordea tendinae and subvalvular apparatus preventing
Prolapse of valve.

It is life giving, inside and out.
It is sacred, between and within.
I will not cage.
I will not harden.
This heart is mine.

CEILING TILES

by Jennifer Barrett

A white, speckled ceiling tile with a brown water stain hangs over my head. I catch sight of it with only a momentary glance, but a flash of recognition draws me back. I lie here, looking up at this splotch, no bigger than my hand and wonder why I should know it so well. In between measured breaths and medical questions, I follow its creeping outline in the corner of this tiny room. The darkness does not hide this subtle feature in the cratered tiles and my pulse rises as I come to terms with why this single detail should be so memorable. I close my eyes and clutch the silver medal around my neck, exhaling a faint prayer. This is the exact stain I stared at almost a year ago when my heart sank, and my naïve expectations faded. My lone focal point was that spot. On that day last year, I could only force glimpses away from it to the slim monitor mounted on the wall in front of me. There on that screen were the blurry black and grey forms of my darling twins, silent and still. I had not even known until that day there were two of you. All these weeks of anticipation, of thoughts filled with joy, were stolen away in that suffocating room. An obscure, aerial spot captured all my focus on that late afternoon. I clung to this dreamy distraction, perhaps because I could not, or did not want to, give my thoughts over to anything else in that room. This drab ceiling tile was my small grip on reality. It was my anchor to the previous minutes when those frightening words had not yet been spoken. It was my touchstone that I was still existing after this incomprehensible news.

I am back in this room, my shirt pulled up to my chest as the ultrasound tech maneuvers a cold gel across my bulging belly. The dimmed lights heighten the effect of the glowing screen, but I look back into the shadows at that ceiling's imperfection, as if by muscle memory. A year has passed, and I am a changed person. My heart has aged. I am not as naïve. I have grieved, found peace, and grieved again. The wand presses and glides over my skin and I take hold of a moment of courage, shifting my eyes to look forward. There is my new life, a beating heart, legs that give a quick kick. I keep watching. He is beautiful. I cling to the rhythmic sound next to my head, keeping time with the pulsing of a tiny heart. Once more I look at that haunting ceiling tile and this time look past it, as if it were a portal into heaven. Pain and love feel inseparable, and in this moment I find myself smiling. With another grasp at my necklace I silently speak to my two children up above and ask them to pray for us, their little brother and me. I am happy to be reminded of their short time on earth. This was the first and last place I witnessed their perfect premature bodies. They left me shortly afterward, but the world marches on and I am still here, doing my part, playing host to each of my darling babies for whatever amount of time, long or short, these little ones are given to me by the Lord, creator of life.

BACKYARD HEROES

by Joel Elwell

Parker finished his breakfast a few minutes after seven, lapping the cold water from his stainless-steel bowl and letting it drip off his muzzle into his food dish. By using this method, he was guaranteed not to miss out on a single molecule of food. Satisfied, he padded to the sliding glass door and scanned the backyard and the fence to the south, but Steve the beagle wasn't out yet. This wasn't unusual, as Steve tended to sleep in until at least seven-thirty on most days, sometimes later. Parker's human, Ed, was still in the shower, so he wouldn't be going out for at least fifteen minutes. He turned around and made his way through the dining room, his nails clicking first on the cool tile, then on the slick wood floor of the front living room. Here he had a great view of the front yard, street and surrounding houses through the large picture window.

As the sun continued to rise over the light blue sky, Parker observed his peaceful neighborhood from the couch that was against the wall adjacent from the window. Leo the oversized cat was laying in the driveway across the street, just below the bumper of a car which parked there every morning. Parker figured that fat black and white blob was going to get squished one of these mornings, but it hadn't happened yet. It wasn't going to be any big loss to Parker if it *did* happen, because Leo was possibly the laziest creature he had ever seen. Once he had even watched a garter snake slip right over the top of Leo's bulging stomach while he sunned himself in the lawn, and the goober hadn't even moved. Parker thought Leo was a real boob, because snakes made some of the best toys.

A mail truck turned the corner and came to a stop three houses away just before a bank of mailboxes. Parker's ears perked up, knowing that it was Davey, the mailman. Davey would continue down the street for a while, his head occasionally bouncing up and down or side to side, listening to a tinny noise that came from the wires he had sticking into his ears. Then he would come back on his side of the street, park the truck and stuff paper in all the boxes on foot. Most of the houses on Parker's side were older and still had the boxes attached to the homes. Parker liked Davey: he was a friend to all dogs, and as a bonus, he delivered treats.

As he watched Davey put mail into their appropriate boxes, movement caught his eye to the north. A man was walking toward Davey, but he was walking in the street, coming up behind Davey's truck. The man didn't look right to Parker; he was walking slow and a little funny, and Parker realized he was trying to hide from Davey. He jumped off the couch issuing a serious warning, and the strange man looked his way. He put a finger to his mouth, puckered his lips and blew towards Parker, then put his hand down. He stared in Parker's direction for a second longer, grinned, and then slipped through the driver's side door of Davey's mail truck.

Parker began barking as loud as he could, and he stood with his paws on the picture window glass. He had to tell Davey there was something wrong, somebody *bad* was now hiding in his mail truck, but Davey couldn't hear him. Those little wires were stuck in his ears.

* * *

Nobody noticed Rodney James Edwards hiding behind the plush green spruce trees on Bishop street, including the mailman starting his route early Monday morning. Edwards looked at his blue uniform, and immediately wanted to kill him. Common sense told him he was just a mail carrier (though he hadn't seen one in almost three years), but the blue uniform was a screaming reminder of the hospital guards. They were the ones that held him down when the white coats shot him full of Haldol or Thorazine when he wouldn't take the pills they told him to swallow. But he had shown them, hadn't he? Doctor Stephanie was never going to give another shot of anything, not to him or anybody else. He laughed a little as he pictured the Iowa Regional Center staff frantically searching the halls and rooms for him while he sat camouflaged behind a row of trees fifty miles away in another state. Nebraska really was the good life, he thought, and this made him laugh harder.

He tried to sit up on his haunches, but the aching pain in his right heel and ankle made him kneel back down. An officer in blue had injured him after he kicked a doctor when he was new to the hospital. He stopped laughing and focused on the mailman who was driving slowly to the next box on the curb. The jackass was bobbing his head back and forth, listening to God knew what through his earbuds. He was just like the guards who stood watch over him in the day yard, giving him no privacy at all. They kept their earphones glued to their heads and waited for him to get out of line. He narrowed his eyes, and was suddenly sure this *was* one of the guards from the hospital. Sure it was. In fact, it was the very officer who had broken his ankle.

When the mailman turned the corner, Edwards crawled out from his hiding place and began following after the man in blue. The truck stopped in front of some duplexes, and the man stepped out and headed for several boxes, his hands full of paper. Edwards stepped into the street and walked behind the jeep, anxious for his opportunity.

A dog began barking at him across the street from behind a picture window, and Edwards stopped and looked at it. He silently told the dog to quiet down and smiled as he started limping to the mail truck again. He felt a happy sort of anxiety rush through him as he slipped into the truck unnoticed.

* * *

Mark Warner was cinching up his tie in the bedroom when the Golden Retriever went crazy from the room down the hall. He loved that dog, but when he got excited about rabbits or squirrels or sometimes just a strong gust of wind, the barking drove him a little nuts. The hound had a thundering voice. He slipped down the hall in his socks, grabbed Parker by the collar and put him out the back door.

It was 7:15.

* * *

Parker trotted over to the fence he shared with Steve and barked three quick times, which was their code. Quick and loud barks outside didn't usually warrant human attention as it would be bad to end up in the Big Metal Cage today. *Very* bad.

Steve poked his head through the dog door, yawned, and came outside. He walked to the fence, shook himself off, and asked Parker what was up with waking him so early. He reminded him that beagles needed more sleep than golden retrievers and all other dogs, except maybe their cousin the basset. Parker apologized and then told him about what he had seen only minutes before.

Steve came up with a few theories about Davey, but Parker logically shot them down. Soon after, they both agreed there was probably concern of foul play. Steve said maybe Duke would be out at lunch time and they could ask his opinion, and they both had a quick laugh about that. Parker was called inside, so they agreed to meet at lunch. Steve went back in his own house in a partial daze to sleep some more.

* * *

At 8:55, Parker was barking his head off in the now empty house just like he was supposed to do when there was trouble. The weird man was on his porch and looking through the window, and there was clearly something wrong with him. The man was wearing Davey's mail coat and making gestures at him with his hands. The coat was stained, and he was smiling. Worst of all, there was no sign of Davey.

* * *

Edwards placed mismatched mail advertisements in the box next to the Warner's house and quickly pressed his hand and face to the window. Just an annoying dog barking to what appeared to be an empty house. He had jammed a screwdriver through the mailman's throat earlier, glowing from the satisfaction of the blood spraying over the letters and magazines in the back of the truck, laughing as the man gasped and tried to scream for help. He could give a rat's ass whose mail he stuck in whose box. The rusty colored dog inside was going crazy, threatening to eat him through the glass, but Edwards only pointed a finger pistol at him, fired, and smiled as he turned around. He whistled as he walked back to his new rolling mail castle, where neither man nor beast could harm him.

* * *

Parker sat at the window all morning, keeping watch for the new fake mailman. Nothing. Finally, at 12:15 that afternoon, THE MAN came back home for lunch.

He made his way to the back door quickly, so the fresh nose prints and slobber wouldn't be noticed on the front window. Luckily, the distraction worked, and he was let outside without question.

When Parker arrived at the fence, Steve the beagle was rolling around on his back, trying to scratch that never reachable itch that every dog has been cursed with. Upon seeing Parker, he jumped to his feet, gave a short howl in greeting, and jogged over to the fence to visit with the young neighbor. They ran up and down the fence, conversing about the morning's events for several minutes before Duke, the great Pyrenees from the yard behind them, came to join in on the conversation. Duke's yard ran perpendicular to the other yards, so he was able to stand at the t-bone intersection of the fences and talk with both dogs. They invited Duke to jump the fence into one of their yards (something he could easily do and actually often did), but he declined. Apparently, he had already been scolded for smashing the cat a good one, and didn't want to be yelled at again. He said he loved that cat, but sometimes just whomping him on the head with his gigantic paw when the cat was relaxing was just too hard to pass up.

Steve told Parker that he had indeed been aware of the dirt-bag mailman imposter who was undoubtedly up to no good. Steve said he could smell trouble right through the screen door, and where the hell was Davey, who pitched him a treat when he was outside?

Parker, who was rarely outside when Davey came by to pitch treats, (but he did leave one inside the mailbox once in a while) said he didn't know where Davey was, but he was sure the new guy was planning on killing him.

Duke, who weighed about one-forty, said he usually got two or three treats, and who were they talking about again? Oh yeah, Davey. Parker liked Duke, but he wasn't the quickest dog on the block. When it came to muscle, however, Duke was your dog.

Steve, who had a way of explaining things even Duke could understand, summarized from what Parker had seen earlier and the strong odor he had smelled through the door, that Davey was either hurt badly, or already dead. With no treats delivered anywhere, Parker sadly agreed and Duke asked once more who they were talking about. Before they could remind him, he charged after a rogue squirrel in the neighbor's yard and crashed into the chain link fence. The squirrel chattered and cursed at Duke, but he just laughed and asked if the squirrel had seen Davey. The squirrel said something else that only squirrels can understand, and then vanished up a tree.

Parker rolled his eyes and told Steve he thought Duke had another concussion. He started to call after Duke but was summoned inside, so he let it go. Steve briefly studied his giant friend who was now gnawing on a steel fence post, and then went about trying to scratch his back again.

* * *

Duke's master was a beautiful forty-something brunette, and she tried to walk him on her lunch break as often as she could. At 1:10, she hooked his horse-lead to his collar. He had proven long ago that he could break any regular dog leash.

"Come on, Bubba," Kathy Ziehoff said. Duke was already pulling her to the door, catching her off guard. "Hold on, Duke!" She pulled back on his leash, but he had already bounded out and was dragging her alongside the screen door. Kathy yanked back as hard as she could, which brought Duke to a slow pause. He gave an encouraging woof, trying to explain that his might was probably needed now more than ever. Kathy had time to pull the door shut, and then Duke was pulling her down the drive and onto the sidewalk, forcing her to jog to keep him from ripping her shoulder from its socket. Once she got even with him, she came to a stop and yanked back with all her strength. Grudgingly, Duke stopped and sat down.

"I don't know what the problem here is, but if you can't walk nice and behave yourself, we're going home. Is that what you want?"

They started off again at a slower pace, and Kathy praised him often. He was able to walk at a normal pace for only a few minutes before he started pulling slightly harder and harder. He couldn't stop himself - he was sure that his friends needed his help.

"Last chance, big guy. I'm warning you. If you keep this up, you'll spend the afternoon in the kennel."

* * *

Edwards succeeded in claiming two more victims in the neighborhood before heading back towards the house with the angry red dog. He had decided to kill that dog because, well, he didn't really know why. He decided by this point, he didn't really need a reason. The two victims he offed had been passed out when he entered the shack of a house, and the murders were too easy for him, giving little satisfaction.

Three other houses were empty, (it was amazing how many people left their front doors unlocked) and a fourth house had presented a small but infuriating problem: a chihuahua with little dog syndrome.

As soon as he entered the house, the little orange dog charged, startling him so much that he dropped the screwdriver he was holding on the hardwood floor. He kicked at the little barking freak, but instead kicked the screwdriver under a reclining chair. This particular chair also happened to be the favorite hiding place of said barking (and now very angry) freak. He got down on all fours and reached blindly under the chair for his weapon of choice, and that's when the little fucker bit him on the hand.

* * *

In a bedroom down the hall, seventy-six-year-old Mable Fenster woke from the light nap she'd been taking. She started to call out to her Cracker Bear to stop barking at the neighbors, then snapped her mouth shut when she heard a man's voice. She picked up the phone and dialed 911.

A calm female voice answered on the first ring. "Nine-one-one, what is your emergency?"

"There's a maniac in my house," Mable whispered. "He's trying to kill my Cracker!"

"Calm down, ma'am. Who is in your house?"

"I don't know!" Mable covered her mouth, but she was almost screaming in a loud, hoarse whisper. "It's a man, and I think he's trying to kidnap or kill my Cracker Bear!"

"I can't understand you, ma'am. Are you at 2129 north fifty-first street? Just whisper yes or no if -"

"Yes! Yes! Yes!" Mabel, crying now, dropped the phone and crept to her door, head cocked to one side and listening to her precious Cracker snarl and bark in the other room.

"Ma'am? Ma'am? Sergeant, I've got a hysterical elderly female, claiming a maniac bear is stealing her crackers. I think she dropped the phone. She's sobbing in the background."

Had Mable been listening, she would have heard a male voice in the background advising to stay on the line, alert animal control and dispatch officers, code three.

* * *

Edwards cried out, drawing his hand back at once, and tipped the chair over with his other hand. He saw the screwdriver and grabbed it just as el loco chihuahua lunged at him again and bit his other arm, its needle teeth ripping the skin off as it retreated. He stood up, panting and uttering unintelligible sounds, kicking at the dog again. This time the mutt ran under a couch, and Edwards started towards it until he heard muffled screams from a room down the hall. The freak of nature under the couch was emitting a constant snarling growl that he might have normally associated with a wolverine. He turned and stormed out of the house, leaving the front door wide open.

Good, he thought. *I hope the little shit follows me out and gets run over by a mail truck.* Thinking of the mutt getting squashed by a truck of any kind struck him as extremely funny, but a mail truck really tickled him. Soon he was laughing out loud, forgetting all about the fresh wounds the furry orange tornado had inflicted on him. Blood was running from his hand, and it covered the Phillips he was carrying, lubricating his grip. He didn't notice.

As he walked down the sidewalk (he had abandoned the mail truck in an alley several blocks ago), he realized he was back to the beginning of his route. *"My route,"* he said out loud, and at first it startled him. He hadn't spoken a word in over two years since he decided to stop talking to his psychologist, his psychiatrist, *and* his counselor. They weren't helping him—couldn't help him—not as long as they continued to think there was something wrong with his mind.

How does it make you feel to look at this picture of your mother, Rodney?

What kinds of feelings do you have towards your sisters, Rodney? Draw a picture with this crayon that would represent your current emotions, Rodney.

Why do you think you still want to hurt women, Rodney? Did Doctor Stephanie say something that bothered you before you hit her? How do you...what do you...

why do you...

He shook his head wildly, hoping the agitation would still the voices.

"Got what she deserved!" He would answer all their questions now, by God. "I hate her, and her, and black inside, and I'm glad she's dead, and they all should die! All...should...*die!*" He was shouting at this point, not knowing or caring if anyone could hear him. A dog was howling, and he couldn't tell at first if it was real or in his head.

By the time he stopped walking, he was standing with a sticky, blood coated screwdriver in his hand, looking at the front of the house with the crazy dog that had tried to blow his cover this morning. More howling, and now sirens going off, and—

"Who cares?" Edwards said aloud again. Everything was probably in his head, and who cares, because he would just kill everyone and everything.

He was standing on the porch now, and after he slipped the screwdriver in his pocket, he placed his hands around his face so he could see through the window, and again all he saw was a fleabag dog crawling off the couch, snarling at him. He pulled away, and the blood on his palms left a smeared and unpleasant stain on the glass, one that rivaled the dog's drool from the inside.

He would kill everything, starting with the noise maker inside. After that, he would go back and eliminate the scruffy orange thing that had bit him, and wipe out its owner for allowing such a poor excuse for a dog to exist. With all that decided, the stress deserted him and he started giggling with excitement again.

* * *

The howling from next door woke Parker from his early afternoon nap at 1:15, and he lifted his head and ears in full alert.

At first all he saw was a young rabbit hopping into his front yard. Poor Steve, he thought. Those rabbits always had it out for him. Of course, Steve had murdered quite a few of them, but still. He laid his head back down, then suddenly saw the no-good murdering mailman imposter sneaking onto his porch. He tried to be quiet, but a low, angry growl was escaping from him. He went slinking off the couch and low crawled to the front door. As he went, Parker saw that the impostor was carrying a dark colored object in one hand, and he had more stains on his shirt, pants and hands.

The man was talking out loud to no one...and giggling.

* * *

Duke looked down at his paws, feeling guilty and anxious at the same time. He couldn't go back home, not with a no-good non-biscuit giving Davey Killer in the area. Still, he had to slow down a little, or his master would get mad. But when they turned the corner onto Steve and Parker's street, he stopped. The fake mailman was walking up Parker's lawn toward the house, carrying something in his hand and shouting at someone, though Duke could see no one else around. The deepest, ugliest growl came out of his throat, and Kathy looked down at him, startled.

"Easy, Duke," she said, looking around with eyes wide.

Duke's lips peeled back over his exposed teeth, his growl blending with a fierce whining snarl of hate.

He shot off toward the man, who was now on Parker's porch. Kathy was not prepared for this, and Duke jerked her off her feet. He dragged her for about ten feet on her side, and she cried out in pain before giving up her grip on his leash and letting him go. Somewhere in the distance, sirens were heading in their direction.

* * *

Parker stayed hidden behind the front door, his growl now at a level that would have warned any normal idiot of certain death. The locked door knob above him rattled back and forth, and he prepared himself for the door to swing open. Instead, he saw the man's figure move in front of the picture window, putting his face and hands up to the glass to look inside like he had done this morning.

Parker backed up, ready to charge the glass when he saw Steve the beagle running in from the left side of the yard, growling and howling at the same time. He didn't have time to wonder how Steve got out, because at that moment, a white and brown blur was charging in from the right.

* * *

Duke had gotten his speed up to twenty miles an hour when he reached the porch and leaped at the bad man. The man was looking the other way at Steve, who sounded angrier than Duke had ever heard him. Duke opened his great jaws, said hi to Steve cheerfully in midair, and closed his teeth around the bad man's neck. His force shattered the picture window and pushed them through and onto the wood floor. Glass exploded in every direction, and Duke was cut badly on his snout. Still, he did not let go of the bad man.

Edwards screamed out in pain and surprise as he went through the glass, first smashing and then cutting the left side of his forehead and cheek. As he hit the floor, a hundred- and forty-pound furry alien landed on top of him, pushing most of the air out of his lungs. He tried to force air back in, but the thing on him was crushing his chest and tearing his throat open with its insanely huge teeth. He swung his fists wildly at the beast, but it would not let go. Blood began pumping out of his neck from the cruel opening, saturating his shirt and turning the large white and brown dog a reddish-pink color. The screwdriver had disappeared during the collision, and he felt around blindly for it. Instead, he picked up a four-inch shard of glass and started to swing the weapon at his aggressor. A new sharp pain stopped him mid swing.

The original mutt he wanted to kill had clamped its teeth down over his right hand, making the glass twist in his grip. The reddish demon disguised as a retriever was breaking the bones in his knuckles – he could feel them grind – and as he dropped the shard of glass, it slit open the meaty part of his first two fingers, severing the tendons.

Operating on pure adrenaline, Edwards brought his left knee up and drove it into Duke's side. The dog cried out and unwillingly let his death grip go, then slid off his chest and onto his left arm, panting and wheezing his breath in and out in quick bursts. With his right hand still secured in the stupid red dog's mouth, he kicked at it with his left leg.

New pain jolted into his left shin and calf, and when he raised his head to look down, he saw the stupid beagle from next door had ripped through his blood-stained pants and was apparently trying to detach his entire muscle. Instinct told him to kick the little bastard with his other leg, but that was when something punctured his testicles with miniature ice picks.

The insane chihuahua that attacked him earlier had latched onto his balls, playing tug-of-war with them. Edwards began screaming, then howling, and when the chihuahua freed one of his testicles from its protective sack, the pitch became too high for any human to hear. The blood loss and pain were too extreme to bare: his muscles relaxed, his vision faded, and he gave up his struggle.

As police cruisers pulled up with lights and sirens adding to the almost unbearable canine chorus coming from inside the house, Kathy stepped through the shattered window, crunching the broken glass as she knelt down beside her dog. As she stroked Duke's blood drenched coat, tears fell onto his ears as she whispered to him, begging him to survive. His breathing slowed somewhat, and he didn't sound quite as labored with each breath. Still, she was sure she would lose him.

The police arrived just before Animal Control, and Kathy immediately put her hands in the air as the officers rushed the house with service weapons drawn. She explained what she knew of the situation, (which was practically nothing), and told them there was a dead man inside the house. An officer stepped through the destruction and identified Rodney James Edwards, the escaped psychopath from Iowa. Donning a pair of blue latex gloves, he made a quick check to the man's neck and declared Edwards deceased. Animal control was cleared to approach the scene, and they carefully loaded Duke in their truck via stretcher. They rushed him and Kathy to an emergency vet, leaving the police officers completely puzzled as to what had taken place.

Mable Fenster arrived as other Animal Control vehicles were coming and going, desperately looking for her dear sweet Cracker Bear.

Parker and Steve had both let go of Edwards on their own, but officers had to carefully remove Cracker from the dead man's crotch. She had almost severed both testicles, and they were unable to find one of them.

"Apparently Cracker has been snacking in between meals," an officer said, handing the snarling pooch to Mabel. She whisked the snaggletooth gremlin away from the man, paying no attention to him. She was far too busy sobbing and smothering her sweet, precious Cracker Bear to be bothered by irrelevant details.

* * *

The leaves were turning red and gold on the neighborhood trees when the three dogs were finally able to gather again at the chain linked fence. Parker and Steve had met daily since the incident, but Duke had three broken ribs, so he had been let out in the front yard for a while to keep him from getting too excited around his friends. He was close to a hundred percent now, but he wore a protective canvas vest just to play it safe. Steve told Duke he looked like a canine football player, and Duke grinned with pride.

Steve said he had actually been praised for jumping through the screen to help his friends. Parker told them that he had gotten plenty of compliments and attention, but was still occasionally scolded for putting nose prints on the new glass window. Duke thought that was great and said he was hungry. He told them his master had labeled him a hero, but he had no idea what that meant, so he had scrambled after the cat and he too was scolded. Soon, the three decided that a canine neighborhood watch was probably in order, so Steve said he'd see what he could do.

Cracker lived several houses down, and while she was absolutely *not* allowed to come visit, they could hear her high pitch and somewhat annoying bark most days, and all three sent hellos in return.

The orange sunset was slipping away from them, and soon Duke and Parker were called inside. They said goodbye, and as he went in, Parker looked back to see Steve roll over and try to scratch his back again.

THEY ARE DOING IT DOWN THERE - FOOTBALL

by Dean Hyde

It had been a tough week at work. Computer systems only crashed three times. That was the production system. The test system crashed Five! As a tester, that tells me that something in one of the builds was moved thru change control before it had been thoroughly tested. New test scripts even had errors in them. One of the testers had no experience with any kind of production system. Who hired this guy? Must have some dirt on somebody in the hiring chain.

Traffic was bad too. Just made it in time to check in, go through the security check, and make it to the gate as the last person to board. Ten planes ahead of us. Finally, in the air as it started to get dark. I slept for the first hour.

My flight was headed west. It barely kept up with the edge of darkness. From the air, cities and small towns lit up. Since it was Friday, the brightly lit ovals for the small-town football fields dotted the landscape. Looking down, I knew that they were doing it down there. But just what was it...

Coach Rosco was about to be caught between the tackling dummy sled and the goal post. Third game of the season was coming up. The injury list was growing. The biggest lineman blew an ACL in the last play of the last game. Which of course they lost. Pulled hamstrings and groin injuries had taken out four other first stringers. The main quarterback was kind of iffy. Rumor had it he had knocked up the Captain of the cheerleading squad after the junior/senior prom last spring and might have to drop out of school and get a job to support a wife and baby. He was a junior (now a senior) and she was a sophomore and would be a junior if it wasn't for the fact that she threw up in class every morning. Her dad was the Superintendent of Schools. Can you see the pressure this put on the coach?

Coach had to win this next game. Last year was a 5 and 7 year and before that was 6 and 6. Another losing season and he would be out of a job. He would have to leave the state to get another teaching job. Texas really likes its football. They don't like losing coaches or losing seasons for very long.

Jamie, the long-haired, blond tennis coach had just started her second year at the same school. The tennis team won the district title and placed second at state. This was her second year of teaching and she had done well. Her reward was to be allowed to attend several clinics for tennis coaches during the summer. Big cities like Dallas, Ft Worth, and San Antonio hosted some of the clinics.

The local school board still had hopes last summer that Coach Rosco might turn in a winning season. He had been a coach for a long time. He just might need a refresher about some football techniques. So, they sent him off to a few coach's clinics during the summer. Coincidently, the dates and locations for the tennis and football clinics matched. Even the clinic hotels.

When the coaches turned in expense reports and hotel bills, no one noticed that the two coaches were in adjoining rooms. No one else knew that they were in connecting rooms.

Almost game time. Coach Rosco finished the locker room pep talk and led the team out to the field. Jamie sat with the rest of the faculty in the stands. She stood up yelling and cheering for the coach when he ran by. Coach Rosco waved back and smiled at Jamie.

Starters are normally determined the day before the game. Coach Rosco had struggled with this for a week, knowing the sad shape some of the players were in. His team won the toss and elected to receive. Coach made his final pick and sent the team onto the field. Three and out and they lost the ball. The other team scored. The first quarter continued the same way. Trading the ball and no score.

Second quarter and two players got hurt and had to leave the game. Second string players were being added to the line on both sides. Just before half time, the other team scored.

Third quarter, the home team scored and made the extra point, tying the game.

Fourth quarter the other team scored again and missed their extra point. The clock ticked on. The home team quarter back took a hard hit and a broken leg. Second string quarter back hardly knew which end of the ball to point down the field when he threw it. Surprisingly enough, he threw a pass to the end zone which was caught by a third string receiver. Game still tied.

Coach Rosco hoped and prayed for the extra point. The ball was snapped.

Bing, bing, bing. "This is your Captain speaking. We are on the final approach to DFW. Please put the tray tables back. Put you your seats in the upright position and prepare for landing."

THE JOINT

by Fred Snowardt

Started while small
Just tagging along for fun
Babysitting cost money
Either way wasn't my call

They said it was for relaxing
Socializing more likely
Beer was the moderator attraction
Conversation made life less taxing

Long necked bottles were all you got
Nurse it along was their goal
No intentions to get drunk
Only a buzz was sought

Juke box would sing
Pool balls were clicking
Shuffle board pucks a-crashing
A couple doing a country swing

Honky Tonk was the sway
With a little country mixed in
Six plays for a quarter
Can't get that bargain today

Allowance was a quarter
Big money back then
Go check out the latest comics
Handling the money like a hoarder

Turn the pages of the comic book
Read sheets fast as could
Counter person didn't want you lingering
Soon would get that "look"

Time to pick out the best
After all was a whole nickel
Then off to the five and dime
Hot Spanish peanuts top of the list

No fear of predators on street
Lots of folks on the walks
Big night on the town
Go inside in case of heat

Saturday night the town would rock
Bands playing old time country
Folks dancing and laughing
With different venues of talk

Boys looking and driving main
Girls walking sidewalks hoping
Romance was in the air
Sometimes in vain

Little money left, no advance
Could save it till later
Maybe a soda
Burning a hole in pants

Buy a large bottle we learned
Only size available
Back then only five cents
Get two cents returned

Some called it beer hall
Others a saloon
We named it a beer joint
Whatever the call

Clock would get late
Eyelids were drooping
Curl up in a vacant booth
Catnap during the wait

Responsibilities were none
Not a care in the world
Keep out of mischief
Stay the trouble free one

Had no idea when
They'd call it a night
Supposed to close at midnight
Life at the joint was good back then

FOREVER MISSING YOU

(A Song by Mary Baker)

(ch)
Don't even know why, I can't even see, these tears in my eyes, they must be blinding me.
Don't know why they just, don't move away, I'm afraid that this heartache, is here to stay.

(v1)
And I can't fight the problem - I can't fight the pain
It hurts even now to see the letters of your name.
And I wonder at night, as I drift off to sleep,
Is my wound superficial, or is it way too deep

(v2)
Are my longings just longings, that cannot be fed
have these emotions I'm feeling, overtaken my head
When my thoughts go astray, like a leaf in the wind,
Your face comes before me, and haunts me once again.

(ch)
Don't even know why, I can't even see, these tears in my eyes, they must be blinding me.
Don't know why they just, can't leave me alone, I'm afraid this heartbreak, has found a home.

(v3)

Though I can't understand it, or make it go away,
I'll look toward the future, and to a much brighter days
As the pain finally dies, and my wounds finally heal
I'll work harder than ever, to make my nerves like steel

(v4)

Though it might not help, or hold back the tears,
Maybe the pain won't destroy me, or fulfill all my fears.
I'll just smile at the moon, and say good night to the day
And close down the curtains, like at the end of play.

(v5)

This love affair may be over, but another's around the bend
And maybe with his help, my heart will finally mend.
But until that day, I'll continue to dry my eyes
Because my heart still chases you, and wants you to be mine.

(ch)

Don't even know why, I can't even see, well these tears in my eyes, they must be blinding me.
Don't know why they just, don't leave me alone, I'm afraid that this heart, has turned to stone

I AM A CHRISTIAN WARRIOR

by Mary Baker

Why is it that I, because I am a Christian
I am "required" to bow to everyone else's religion
but if I mention my Christianity, I am the one being offensive

As a Christian military veteran, I'll tell you what is offensive
It is offensive that I am forced to tolerate everyone else's behavior
no matter how immoral or offensive it is
while anything I do is not tolerated at all, even if it is moral and right

It is offensive to me that when I am violated, or
I disagree with a person's behavior, I must not speak my opinion
because it must be my "Christianity" talking
not just me as a person of character, integrity, morals, and dignity

It's offensive that "my religion" is said to be offensive to everyone else
but it is the same religion this county was founded upon
it is the basis of our moral code and conduct that was once the grounding for
our nation

It is offensive to me that I am told I can't say Merry Christmas
when that is exactly what the holiday is all about,
it is Christmas and I am Merry about it, but I can't share the real Joy with anyone
because it may offend others and their "right" to days off, for a holiday they don't
even believe in

It's offensive to me that all other religions and spiritual paths
receive freedom of religion and speech
while my Christianity is chained and muzzled on a daily basis
and even censored to ensure my voice is stifled amidst the chaos

It is offensive to me that other religions can boldly proclaim
their views and beliefs at the top of their lungs
but I am required to whisper my views
so hopefully no one will hear, and be offended

It's offensive to me that my religion provided the pot
that all others who came to our country melted in
and now they ridicule the very land I protect for them to reside within.

It is offensive to me when others want to defame our money
and remove the words "In God We Trust"
For when we truly lived that way as a country, we were not in deep debt
like we are today, as a dollar was actually worth something back then,
not just because of what it could buy, but because of what it stood for

It's offensive to me that the Ten Commandants are so burdensome
that they must be removed from our courthouses and halls of justice,
but if we truly lived those ten phrases, we would not need to use those houses
and halls

It is offensive to me that I can defend my country and fight for your freedom of
religion but that freedom does not apply to me
and if I tell you of how God rescued me in that fox hole or how he led us through
the mine field unharmed, or how he kept our shot-up fighter jet from leaking
fuel, you call me a lunatic and say I'm offending you

It's offensive to me that when I come home from my third
or fourth or sixth tour of duty, you still expect me to blindly follow
the crowd that has been forming while I was gone
You expect me to tolerate everything that I don't believe in and yet
none of my beliefs are "allowed" anymore in the country I so dearly love

It is offensive to me that I cannot defend my religion
because if I do, I am the one being offensive
Funny, I thought I was the one being tolerant to everyone else all along
I just wish they would be tolerant of me and my religion for a change
It's a right I have fought for, and I'm sure I've earned it,
offensively or not.

ADRIFT

by Mary Baker

Disconnected, ever moving
But never going forward
Apart, back to back
Living separate lives together
Awash, out of synch
Oil amidst troubled waters
Broken, hearts divided
Ties unable to mend
Valleys, words unspoken
Breathe and exhale, again
Oceans, waves swaying
Tides that carry emotions
Frustration, double meaning
Turn and plod away
Sadness, ever heavy
Keeping broken souls at bay
Flooded, going under
Ropes slipping from grasps
Distant, space evolving
Enveloping heart and soul
Foreshadowing, once predicted
Told of challenges unknown
Alcohol, numbing senses

Dulled, but ever present
Threads, frayed and broken
Tying knots without ends
Silence, loudly spoken
Shouting across the room
Stifled, ever protruding
Understanding hidden beneath words
Hearts, carelessly beating
Hardened by forbidden sin
Separate, but together
Moving cautiously against the wind

CHOCOLATE

by Cindy Cronn

It's in the freezer. Right now. I can go to the freezer, open the box, and eat just one. Just one piece of chocolate that was not pretty enough to put in a gift box of Russell Stover's. I know I can eat just one.

I open the box. It is a jumble of pieces of candy, occasionally losing their stuffing, but they look fine to me. They are not nested in the standard tiny brown pleated cups, these rejects of the assembly line. It is impossible to tell what's inside each one because there is no label identifying their contents. But I never met a piece of chocolate I didn't like. Yes, even coconut. I love the stuff. I am only going to have one.

I choose my first, er my one. It is oblong with a design in relief on its top. I open my mouth and bite down, cleverly realizing that these things have been frozen, but believing in the power of teeth that have stood the test of time. I get nowhere. The chocolate morsel is, well, frozen. But I know the miracle of the microwave and I place the piece of candy all by itself inside on the rotating glass tray. I set the timer for 5 seconds and then 10, knowing that the results will be oozing with chocolaty goodness. And I am right! Though it is a little hot, what must have been intended as a chewy nougat is a soft indescribable wad of sugary soft toffee-like candy with a melty chocolate drizzle. Delicious. But I am only having one.

Well, maybe two.

I eat the second one, also given the microwave treatment. And this one is a chocolate soft centered delight, my favorite when I was a child. I wonder at the miracle of the microwave that was not available when I was growing up. I don't suppose it would really be necessary if the candies weren't frozen, but I am thinking it is a pretty nice addition, one I may continue should I ever be fortunate or loved enough to receive a box of chocolates not called "Bloopers".

The box still looks pretty full. Will my friends notice if I eat just one more? I promised that I would keep these frozen for our next meeting and believed, at the time, that I was strong enough to fulfill that commitment. They will never know if I have a third little nibble. I look for one that is different from the two I have already eaten. There must have been a run on faulty nougats at the Russell Stover's factory. I fumble through the box and find one of a different shape. It may be a chocolate soft center, but I love those and could eat a whole box … No. I could NOT eat a whole box. I care about my health. I try to exercise. I know how a sugar high creates a cycling low. I could NOT eat a whole box. But this little piece will not be missed in the jumble. I place this piece in the microwave, well actually two pieces because it is wasteful to use that microwave energy on just one piece of chocolate. Besides, 10 seconds on 2 pieces might avoid the slight oozing problem encountered in the first experiment. I enter 10 seconds on the number pad of the microwave and listen to it hum. I look inside to see if all is well and see that the two companions turning slowly on the rotating plate are not oozing, just warming perfectly.

I eat them, pretty much without thinking, because if I thought about it, my inner critic would be shaking her head at me, disgusted by my lack of self-discipline. I do begin to equate four pieces of chocolate candy with a standard candy bar which I would never allow myself if I was standing in the checkout line at the grocery store eyeing the tempting display to my right. But is that so bad? A candy bar? Actually this might be a little less than a candy bar. I'll just have two more. Warmed in the microwave, of course. That is really not as necessary now because the candy has thawed to some degree.

I look at the box. It seems like it might be noticed by my friends that there is a little less candy there. Probably they won't remember or care. So I think now that I have had a candy bar, I will just put the box back in the freezer and ignore it for the 28 and a half days I have to wait until the next meeting.

It's Wednesday, two days after my pledge to freeze the candy for our next meeting. It was Deron's fault! He brought this box to my house! I didn't know before this week that there was such a thing as a box of Bloopers. I haven't had any chocolate since yesterday afternoon. There were the three pieces I ate when I returned from my bike ride, but they don't count because I rode 40 miles to Fort Calhoun and back. Each hill was worth at least one piece of candy.

I'll just have one. Or two. Well, I'll see how I feel. I think six equals a candy bar and I have done a lot of yard work. My stomach aches a little and is a bit unsettled, but I think that was from the seafood I had last night for dinner. I shouldn't eat seafood on a full stomach.

You know these candies aren't really that good. They are not pretty. I have no way of knowing what I'm getting, but it seems like they are all the same, the product of a messed up nougat line. I will eat a couple of the more disfigured ones and search around for something else in the box that is different from the ones I have already eaten.

There really isn't much variety here. I really should stop. But it's chocolate and there might be a chocolate shortage … sometime.

That does it! I have to stop. It's Thursday morning and I can't put that box of chocolates out of my mind. I'm sure this is an addiction and I am equally sure that there is not a support group for someone who can't leave a box of Russell Stover's Bloopers alone.

I'm throwing them away. This solution has to be one of the Twelve Steps. I am getting rid of them as soon as I have just one more. Well, two.

There. They are in the bottom of the wastebasket. I'll toss my coffee grounds in on top of them … just for good measure. I won't acknowledge the image of myself digging through the garbage for a piece of chocolate now surrounded by plastic wrappers and cornhusks. I won't!

I'll buy a replacement box for the next meeting. I will only have to eat a little of that box.

FOR SUCH A TIME AS THIS:
How Living with an Obsessive Compulsive Disorder Mother Prepared Me for a Pandemic

by Robrenna Redl

"Don't forget to put bleach in that dishwater." Bleach in the dishwater was a requirement my mother assigned us each time we washed the dishes. For her, there were many requirements for keeping a home clean. It looked as if no one ever used it: shiny and white. The dishes and silverware were sparkling enough to see our reflection. The glasses were spotless. As a ten-year-old, washing the dishes was a stressful chore. I knew when it came time for my mother to inspect, if the dishes weren't to her standard, every plate, fork, cup, and spoon would end up back in the sink for a re-wash.

When I was in tenth grade, I took a psychology class. I found it fascinating to learn how the brain works, and the effects of familial relationships, life experiences, and trauma determined certain behaviors in people. As I read about "Obsessive-Compulsive Disorder," my mother's face slowly appeared on the page. I whispered to my- self, "Oh my goodness, that's my mother."

The National Institute of Mental Health defines Obsessive-Compulsive Disorder (OCD) as a common, chronic and long-lasting disorder in which a person has uncontrollable, reoccurring thoughts (obsessions) and/or behaviors (compulsions) that he or she feels the urge to repeat over and over[1].

After school that day, I sat at the kitchen table to do my homework. I opened by psychology book and said, "Mom, I want to read something to you." She stood

---

1 *https://www.nimh.nih.gov/health/topics/obsessive-compulsive-disorder-ocd/index.shtml*

at the sink, cleaning vegetables and said, "Okay." I read the definition of OCD to her, then looked at her and said, "That's you."

She smiled. "You think so?" she asked. I don't think she took me seriously; to her, it was business as usual.

Later in life, I joined the Texas Army National Guard to help pay for college. When I went to Advanced Individual Training (AIT) to learn my military job skill, I lived in a six-person room with other female soldiers. As we prepared for inspection, I instinctively took the lead on how to clean and arrange our belongings. When the commander came to inspect the room, he stooped down and slid his hand under the radiator; he rubbed his index finger and his thumb together. As he stood up, he shook his head and stated, "This is the cleanest room I've ever inspected." From then on, I became the room commander.

As room commander, it was my job to ensure the room was clean, orderly, and dress-right-dress. Everything was in its place according to the Standard of Operating Procedures Handbook of the Barracks[2]. My mother's OCD teachings came in handy in the military. For six weeks, we received the honor of the Best Room.

My mother's primary fear is with germs and fear of contamination; her compulsion is extreme cleanliness. She keeps bleach in the trunk of her car. She never uses hand towels, only paper towels to dry her hands. Most things she does seem ordinary but, eventually, go to the extreme. Her typical requirements are shoes off at the door, remove "outside" clothes when home, and clean with bleach. On grocery shopping day, be prepared to wipe items off with a disinfecting wipe. Remember to insert certain things, like pancake mix and flour, that go in the pantry in plastic storage bags. The system she has in her kitchen is one where stations have designated functions. For instance, the counters by the sink are for clean dishes only. The counter by the stove and the table is the only place that food can be set or prepped. Cups that have been drunk from must be put in the sink, not on the counter, even if the cup will be used again. The one exception to this rule is the cup can be placed on the table as long as it's not on the same side as food. If this procedure isn't followed, it causes my mother's anxiety level to increase, which displays through anger.

I knew of my mother's obsession with germs, cleanliness, and ritual, but I didn't know her story until I was much older. My mother's life is a snapshot of

---

2 https://www.housing.army.mil/Documents/FSBP2020.pdf

abandonment, multiple sexual assaults, teen pregnancy, and physically abusive relationships. She shared the fears and anxieties that most mothers have but are exacerbated by concerns that black mothers have. Will my child be treated fairly? Will my child receive a quality education? Will my child live to adulthood? Will my child live? These fears and anxieties manifested themselves in keeping her children safe, even if it caused us to fear her. My mother's primary emotion was fear, which showed itself in anxiety and anger. As children, we didn't realize the irritation was entirely directed at us, but for us. When I moved out and lived with two roommates, they were quick to point out that I vacuumed every day after work, and chastised me as I cleaned and dumped ashtrays with a house full of people during a party we threw. I knew what path the obsession would take, so I trained myself to be clean but not obsessively so.

* * *

As I grew older and became a wife and a mother, I maintained a clean, neat, and orderly home, but I was comfortable with not thinking about outside germs as much. When my children were smaller, we would load up the car for a family road trip twice a year to visit my mother in Texas. Because she was a great cook and baker, I always imagined her upside-down pineapple cake or sweet potato pies would be the scent my kids would associate with her. I would learn that it would not be the case. When we went to visit a friend in a rehab center, the smell of bleach smacked our nostrils as soon as we walked through the door. "It smells like Granny's house!" my children exclaimed. The unexpected irony was that the smell of bleach instead of sweet potato pie or upside-down pineapple cake was the smell that my children connected with their granny.

* * *

As the COVID-19 pandemic sent a wave of illness and death to different parts of the world, we were all in shock that this mist, moving through touch and particles in the air, left such devastation behind. News reports stated the virus was related to germs and contamination, causing a choking respiratory illness. The recommendation from the medical community was to stay home and if you have to go out, wear a mask, disinfect as much as possible, and wash hands thoroughly and often. My mother is a nurse, so when she taught us to was our hands, front, back, fingers, nails, and end with your wrist. When turning off the sink, use elbows as not to re-contaminate the hands. I instinctively thought I knew what to do. I bought disinfectant spray and wipes, paper towels, toilet tissue, and hand sanitizer. I'm sure many other people did the same thing—many of these items I already had and used, but not every single day.

As I watched the daily updates, as part of my morning routine, I began to wipe the doorknobs, and spray the air and carpet with the disinfectant spray every day before vacuuming. Grocery shopping took longer in and out of the store. As a good Soldier does, I obeyed the markings in the grocery store, I kept my distance and went down the aisles marked like a one-way street. I kept hand sanitizer with me, and as soon as I got in the car, I slathered it on my hands, the cell phone that I had used for my grocery list, and my debit card. I used the leftover sanitizer for the steering wheel. Once I returned home, I took off my shoes, sprayed my purse, washed my hands, and wiped off the groceries the way my mother taught me. Now that my children are young adults and the pandemic has brought out my mother in me, the smell still reminds them of granny's house, but they long for the scent of my infamous monster cookies, instead.

One day, as I'm washing the dishes, six months into the released information of the pandemic, the smell of bleach wafts through the air. I shake my head and feel that ten-year old girl standing at the sink, washing dishes with bleach in the dishwater. This time the stress and anxiety did not come from my mother, but from this living thing we can't see. I chuckle to myself as I realize my mother's disorder and dysfunction prepared me for this time in history. When I call her on the phone, we joke that she was ahead of her time; she laughs and gives me more instructions on how to keep her grandkids safe. My mother still has OCD; the excessive cleanliness thing is easy for her. Now she feels validated, as what she has felt most of her life makes sense to her. As I've grown older, she's revealed even more of her story, and now, it makes sense to me, too.

THORAZINE ZOMBIE

by Cynthia Douglas-Ybarra

It could have happened this way-or maybe I have the details turned around a bit-but I know it was 1982 and I know I was 15. I know because what happened on June 15, 1982 upended my life and changed it forever.

Here is the story as clear as I can recall it.

On Wednesday mornings, after we ended what *they* called breakfast, we would line up outside of the nurse's station to get our medications, one behind the other, shuffling forward, like mechanical clockwork moving in time. Thorazine zombies, the techs loved to say.

Each person would receive a small white cup, for whatever polychrome pills they had been prescribed and one identical cup for water. There never seemed to be enough water to swallow the pills, and they would get stuck in your throat. Once you were able to choke them down, the nurse would examine the inside of your mouth, command loudly, "Lift your tongue and move it side to side," to make sure you weren't stockpiling any for when you finally grew exhausted by this place, this life.

After the med pass, we would file into the basement to meet with the psychiatrists and discuss our individual medical management as a group. I was not there freely or enthusiastically, just one of many, sent here under the pretext of helping me help myself. There was no this or that choice presented, not in the 1980s. This place was the only place for people with a self-destructive bent.

The room resembled one in which an expert might give a panel presentation on the science of madness, or maybe it was just a classroom setting. I don't recall details about the room, really. My memory is like a haze, concealed, my ability to see it clearly and trust it fully is on unstable ground. I liked to imagine the room used for something constructive, something geared toward the living.

The "shrinks" were all men-all white-maybe three or four of them- and they would sit behind a long and wide table with their stacks of folders in front of them-facing their spectators, taking us in, scrutinizing our moods and movements, looking for signs of improvement or failings. Watching, as if we were oblivious to these close attentions. What they didn't realize, I am sure, is that we were also dissecting them. Looking for an opening to get exactly what we wanted. The medication management piece came when they asked how the medications were working for us and if we were having any side effects. That day I asked for Mellaril, a psychotropic drug, which has since been taken off the market. It was found that it could lead to Torsade de Pointes, a polymorphic ventricle tachycardia; a cardiac dysrhythmia that can, and has, lead to sudden death. I had no clue about that when I requested it, and I can safely assert that, honestly, I wouldn't have given one single fuck -I just wanted to see if it could get me high.

Medical Management was where I could play up symptoms and jump from one medication to the other without the desired effect. Never a benzo, never an opioid, never a stimulant, never anything that could get me high or allow a second of escape. That didn't stop me from trying.

And that is how easy it was to get Mellarill.

In 1982, at 15 I was living on the adult psychiatric unit at the Lincoln Regional Center. They sent me here after my second suicide attempt, using another antipsychotic drug that someone had prescribed to me so I could live.

I can't remember how I ended up on the adult unit, but I know my psychologist at the time, advocated for me to be placed there. Maybe it was because, basically, I had been living on my own, receiving a stipend of a couple hundred dollars a month and food stamps from the state of Nebraska. I was their ward. I think it was because I ran from Boys Town so many times that the courts threw up their hands and finally found me more of an independent living situation.

This day was the same as many others until it wasn't. I was in my individual therapy session when my psychologist asked me a bizarre question. Maybe he wanted to break the news to me slowly, or maybe he was just playing a head game -but at some point, in our session on July 15, 1982, he asked how I would feel if someone in my family died. I played along, thinking he was going to surprise me with some big teaching moment. I remember having a kind of typical teenaged response- "I wouldn't care," I said, meaning it to come out flippantly and cold.

Part of me wanted to see a shocked response cross his face. But that never happened. I said it as if saying it would make it truth. At that time, I passed myself off as badass bitch. Stone cold, nobody here is going to break through these walls. The message I sent with a look was, "Stay the hell away or I swear I will stab you." But my true self, the one living inside of my core, wanted to tell a different story. I found out, after many years, to do that I would have to peel away the layers of disappointment, abuse, and self-loathing to get to the center of me.

The phone rang, and he handed it to me. I reached out for it, and it was my mom. Crying. The words came out in sobs. "Your... sister... killed... herself. This was not real; this couldn't be real. He just wants to see how I handle this. But it was real and there was no going back. The words filled my head with images, echoing from one side to the other, over and over again. Asphyxia, hanging, suicide. Asphyxia, hanging, suicide. Asphyxia, hanging, suicide. It took me a while to measure the impact of her death, but I would never again try and take my own life.

POEMS FROM AN ARMY MEDIC 1969-70

Guadalupe J. Mier

A Death in Vietnam
(1974)

Mother, were you weeping
as the wounded sky bled fire
and the banshee's cry
tore through the heavens
sending all your children
and their gods
to the shelter of the caves?

Paint with tears
the unsaid word
that sits on your son's lips –
the world is now the color
of empty eyes.

Child's Gambol (in the early morning)
(1967)

Silly-faced willy-nilly foolish fellows
racing through their butterfly net dreams
across the marsh and meadows:

as the sun's burst places
bright slivers of lemon-drop shine
on their faces,
the cherry red dawn
comes undone.

Do you hear the *cu-cu-ru-cu-cu* of mournful dove?
Can you see them polliwogs, Pauline?
Skip some stones; see them scattering.
Let's play war.
No, let's play love.

On an Asian Wind
(1969)

The canons of death
inscribed on the sandbags
have guided the children of destiny
to look at the system and question the rulers
who like Greek gods at Troy
are playing their game
with human toys

The wealth of a nation
misspent on crusades in faraway countries:
who will determine the price of lost lifes
and the futures of young men
ashamed of the shame that they have survived?

Cool Morning Highlands
(1969)

Cool morning Highlands
shimmer in your phosphor essence
bathed at night by monsoon waters
touched by gentle winds

and speaking
from the green-glowering ground
hear the voices of the dead
who rot beneath the rot of leaves.

The world moves on
as monsoon-strewn the leaf-floats
swirl in and out the river's currents
and I am trapped in this flow of time.

Sunday morning, rising son
(1970)

Are you living in the sun light
dancing frozen in crystal,
sad child with soulful smile?

I cast my voice,
a net of cloud prisms;
my light gathers the colors
of everyone's soul.

The storms of my afternoon
are the scraping of chains on human flesh
and the tearing of nails through godly hands.

Who was watching from the olive grove
with the eyes of dispassionate observer,
the descending chariot?
Swing slow, Iscariot.

My cries light up an angered sky;
they shred asunder the curtain
of my Father's Temple.

Now close my final chapter, sweet asterisk!
I hear the Father call my name.
The sun is darkened by the phoenix
rising, slowly from the flame.

Step into my moment, sad children;
stand with me in freedom
as my spirit leaps with joy!

Monsoon morning
(to LC)
(1969)

Today, I woke up
on the wrong side of the world.
If my disposition doesn't suit you,
how do you think I feel
I have put on the boots of war,
humped the hills,
and felt the chill at night
when darkness covers movement
and sound is magnified
beyond proportion.

My first night out I thought of you.
I didn't know what you were doing
in the sunlit world I used to know;
but I wanted to be watching you
and not this chest high grass
around the camp.

Final silence
(1969)

Smile before I forget what happiness was like
the summer we gathered the clouds together
and saved their silver linings for another rainy day.

We laughed and cried for that one-legged pigeon
that dodged pedestrians
in the downtown valleys of the city
as it pecked at Woolworth popcorn
that missed the mouths of children.

I can accept my fate
and dream a different life to come
if I can only see your smile
and you don't turn away —
for love has lost its meaning.

With rifle always at the ready
we cannot love our fellow man
when his death
at my hand waits
as he steps from forest path
in this lush green highland valley.

But when my final silence comes
I hope to feel your summer smile again.

Granny in Pleiku
(2015)

Broom in hand, she's never introduced
but only pointed at.
That's Granny
in black pajamas and cone hat
whisking away the dust
at the entrance to the base camp clinic,
a somewhat semblance
of near clean.

She leans against the wall and waits
as you pass by.
Her betel'd teeth
give her wrinkled face
the appearance of a grand maw gaping,
with an eel-like tongue in motion
in that darkness as she sings
to herself silent songs only she can hear.

Your boots are caked with drying mud
and the red dust of the highlands
falls in clouds from your fatigues.
As you pass into the clinic,
she sweeps behind you —
a semblance of clean.

A Young Montagnard Woman Bathing
(1969)

1/
Four young Montagnard girls
are bathing in a mountainside pool;
the lesser three cup in their hands
water falling from a mountain ledge.
Centered there, lithe and regal,
she is singing as the water
is carried to be showered over her
from the others' unfurled fingers.

This is a vision
for our base camp patrol,
reminding us that life goes on
as we pass. We will soon be gone.

2/
Brown-skinned girl
in shaded pool,
you touch your face
with watered hands:

the lakes in your palms
spill glistening cascades
that reflect the sun's warmth
on your breasts.

Like ripples from a thrown stone
you move the faces of soldiers
passing in review
in a passing war.

3/
Your voice trips
on vowels –
a broken song rises
that birds of paradise
will secretly carry
in their hearts
until the day there is no war.
In bamboo forests they will sing:

I am child-race:
a smile of mornings breaking,
the eye clear as the mountain brook,
the warm heart of the living meadow.

I reach
to the end of the bird's flight.

I am Jarai!
A laugh loud as the sunset,
the delicate strength of a rice shoot,
the voice of bamboo in the night wind.

I live
for the land, the soul of my people.

4/
Brown-skinned girl,
I see your face
once more as I look back
to Plei Do Bai.

I see the light of life
still dances in your eyes.
If you could see in mine
you would see empty space,

my measured time
and tears from crying.
I did not bring this war
(my war is in my soul);

I've only come
to die.

Moose the Wonder Dog
(2015)

Sgt. Moose, the wonder dog!
Like a dark grey armored knight
he stands with muscles tensed
on daily watch from his favorite site:
a small rampart mound with a view
of the traffic on Normandy Road.

His only duty, self-assigned –
is to be on watch for juicy jeeps
and 2½ ton trucks that he can chase.

Old toothless Moose,
his bark is truly worse;
his voice is but a guttural growl, you see.

But it's in his nature to protect us
and he will gum those tires to death
if you give him the slightest opportunity.

The medics from the nearby Quonset D
have their answers on how to fix what they see.
The guys in Mental Health suggest analysis;
the OR techs prefer bilateral orchiectomy –
just a fast snippity-do-dah to his hoo-hahs
should surely calm down his psychosis.

But once we observe that 2-star General cringe
in the back seat of his passing Jeep, a wince
in fear of fearless Moose,
minds are changed.

Oh good friend Moose,
from all that is evil protect us!
No, he must never be tamed.

Tracers Green
(2016)

A steep and well-worn Montagnard trail
is the easiest way to the top of this rise
as we move quietly in hurried walk
to lessen time of visibility and vulnerability.

Except for Doc and Sgt. Rock,
the soldiers in our patrol are mostly tall,
All-American boys —
the new guy is still rosy-cheeked, clean shaven!
As we climb this incline, slightly hunched
from the weight of our packs, it can only mean
we've added a few more degrees to the lean.

Then from the valley forest below
to our left, comes scattered rifle fire:
bullets tearing through the heavy Monsoon air
just inches above our protective head gear
but for Rock and luckily Doc, a little bit higher.

The tracers green
have painted moistened trails in the air
from a not too distant AK-47 somewhere
down there in the trees but the sniper is unseen.
The men slide off the path in unison
into the rushes below and as each takes a position
their M-16s are now unlocked and ready.
As their "Doc" I remain steady,
quickly walking behind their line
to check for any sign of injury from hostile fire,
or from their slide down the steep incline.

In anticipation of a certain enemy rush
The GIs' eyes keep watch on the scattered brush

for any irregular motion
in the nearby grassy field between the line of trees
and our protected position —
on watch for any movement not from breeze.

Rock signals in the grunt on point, El Greco,
instructing him to select three others he can rely on
and search the forest edge with utmost care
for any sign of sniper there.
I suggest to Sarge that I should probably also go
in case there is a call for "Medic!"
I cannot believe I'm saying what I'm saying.
Rock's response is: "Doc, if there's unfriendly fire,
the rest of us will all rush down; so
there is no need to hurry to become a hero."

As the select team vanishes through the tall grass
and while Sarge makes radio contact with Camp Enari,
Preacher, with open Bible, reaches out to someone higher.
The rest of us hold our positions as we follow the progress
of the chosen, counting the long minutes
until they return or there is an exchange of fire.
Then Sarge will lead us toward the waiting forest.

An hour passes.
Then from the field of grass
we hear El Greco's low whistle
that signals the return of his team.
They report that beneath a tree
there were shell casings on the ground,
but there was no shooter to be seen.

Sarge deduced that it probably was a loner
returning to his hootch in the nearby ville
after serving his VC duty the night before.
Perhaps he saw us trudging up that trail,

like easy targets in a shooting game—
like the one at the Fayette County Fair
where months before I basked in "family fame"
after winning a purple and white "god-damn" Teddy Bear.

Iconic boy on water buffalo
(2018)

Waters spring
from the surrounding mountainsides
trickling down clean and fresh
to fill that natural bowl below,
where checkerboard dikes
built by the local Montagnard tribe
calm the flow –
a place to plant their rice.

Sgt. Rock leads his patrol
in semi-silence, skirting past
the rice bowl where the women
from the nearby ville wade
in still waters
tending their rice shoots.

Voices in sing-song tones
are lifted by the breeze
that easily bends the tips
of the young plants dancing
in wind-kissed movement
reflecting the women's soothing songs.

On the right a nearby path that leads uphill
skirts the paddies, and it is there
we see unmoving, statue still,
a bare-chested boy on water buffalo.
Envision this: a Southeast Asian icon
has come to life

straight from the lower left corner border
of a dark cloth souvenir map
labeled with the header

"In the Memory of VietNam 1969-70".
A map I bought at the PX and sent home
to hang on my wall when I return,
or, if I do not,
for my brother to place in my tomb.

The boy in faded black shorts is motionless
with a rice straw dancing in his teeth
as he sits cross-legged on that broad-backed beast.
His straw cone hat hangs low
on his bare brown shoulders,
as his dark black hair is tousled
by the rising breeze
that earlier kissed the rice below.

If the creature sees us,
he makes no sound or movement.
If the boy sees us (and he does)
he makes no sound or movement,
not even when the "newbie" on our team
like a gentle lady tourist, waves at him.
Rock puts a quick end to the Private's error
with his famous "Stare of the Silent Daggers."

Keeping our distance, we depart from the path
far below the point where the boy and beast stand watch.
Silently wending our way up the nearby hills we disappear,
accompanied only by a soft sound rising in the air:
the breeze-borne "song of rice"
the women shared with the wind.

It isn't long before we hear
the rhythmic sound of a clanging bell
as the iconic boy on water buffalo
directs his beast a little nearer
down the path
to protect the women of the ville.

Ben Het 1969

(1969/2001)

There is a mountain near Ben Het
its peak is scarred
and napalm scorched
like all the others

In the shadows of the evening
with its fringe of bare-branched trees
the mountain reminds me
of a tonsured monk medieval
all clad in drab
waiting for his god to do something

Then air strikes rosary
their decades of "Hail Marys"
on the trail behind/beyond
my Ben Het mountain monk
and break the holy silence
that had enveloped me

Verdant
(2015)

a convergence of forces four
on a low plateau while on military tour
in the province we once knew
as Pleiku

two lines of dots in movement
one long and orderly
glides slowly silent green
with only the whisper of the long grass
brushing fatigues
to announce its presence

the other short and low to ground
is weaving through the underbrush
the leader-mother grunting signals
as those that follow in disarray
squeal their recognition
in porcine play

two single points in total silence
one is the sun approaching apex on its daily path
erasing slowly shadows
while an "other"
also known as "burning bright"
flows fluidly through the tall grass deathly quiet

Base Camp Enari is to the east behind us;
to the west, Cambodia.
At our right a hundred yards away,
their leaves dancing in the warm breeze,
stands a tall line of willow trees,
protectors of the river that flows
in the deep gully behind, below.

In the distance to our left
rise the mountains of the highlands
most familiar to my Army boots.

As Sgt. Rock guides his patrol through the elephant grass,
radioman Johnson says in whisper:
"We'll probably see elephants."
I'm thinking, how odd:
at home in Texas, I never saw crabs in the crabgrass.

Helmets before and behind me
fluidly bobbing in rhythm;
fine-tuned is this patrol.
The unseen El Greco, tall and lean,
brings up the rear.

Wild pig mother, gruntingly guiding her brood,
quickly cuts through a space between
two young privates in camouflage green.
As she squeals, a disorderly squad of scrawny piglets five
race this way and that, disrupting the once fine military line.

One more motherly call
and the last, a laggard, walking slowly
through our ranks, snuffles at the heel of a GI's boot,
then squeaks, as if to say:
"Slow down mom,
I'm coming, I'll come!"
Then he too is gone
with a shrill squeal and a dusty scoot.

Then in the distance we hear a tiger's cough —
yes, hair on the neck does stand on end.
We all are frozen in place even before Rock signals halt.
In this open terrain there is no way to ascertain
just how near or far the tiger is.

Each soldier checks his weapon without hesitation,
turning slowly toward that sound
that lingers, a vocal fog in the air, for much too long.
As we move closer to each other in fearful anticipation,
I now can clearly see El Greco's worried face.

And though each soldier's motions
are but a slow dance
to close the spaces between us,
we all know it is the tiger that makes the choice:
long pig; short pig? both delicious.

Rock speaks in signals that we pass in whisper and sign,
the movement of hands and arms to the next GI in line:
walk slowly toward the trees along the ravine;
while one moves facing forward,
the next in careful backward steps,
watches our behind
as we remove ourselves from harm.

The gully is deep,
too steep to run or even safely walk down
to the slow moving river below.
Rock insists it is safer to slide on our butts
while carefully watching for obstructive saplings.
I place my pack between my legs for crotch protection
and my medic's bag is safest
when held closely to my chest.
As I choose my path of least resistance,
I notice that El Greco, tall and lean,
once again is nowhere to be seen.

The sun has reached its peak:
its heat rays filtering through the leaf-filled canopy.
There is no bright and steady noon-shine
as the light of the sun is transformed, passing through the green.

All around us, the air is now a verdant hue:
I feel like bug forever trapped in emerald crystal stone
sledding, sliding, slipping down alone
as if there's no one else around.

I sense an awakening from what seems
a verdant dream
and as he slides beside me, I hear El Greco:
"I had to watch the rear, *hermano!*"

As the natural color of air returns to the world,
he adds with a wink and a grin:
"I think *El Tigre* caught that last little squealer
about the time our world turned green."

Pieta in black pajamas
(2014/2019)

Tableau'd
on the road,
Kontum to Dak To:

riders crowded in an open-air bus
their hands on faces as silencing parentheses
demarcating mouths
that yearn to moan.

Still, she's alone.
Holding him tightly to her chest
looking heavenward with reddened eyes,
one hand held high to God in tearful supplication,
she reaches out in search of explanation.

Papa-san, with wounded head
pressed to her breasts
that lie flat beneath
her bloodstain moistened
black pajamas, rests.
His sightless eyes stare into darkness blacker
than the brain-stained clothes she's draped in.
His peasant hat, a resting cone
on QL 14,
lies there lonesome,
a bullet-torn hole gaping.

I touch a hand that's lost the warm
and gently pull an arm
out from her grasp
as I search his wrist in vain for arterial flow,
perhaps some whisper of a pulse — Oh God no!
while in my head I sense

I've found
the only rhythm near to him:
the echo of her tears intense
as they fall in heartbeat time
with the gentle Monsoon rain.

* * *

and the ants danced
they sensed the scent
through the cleansing rain
of brain parts splattered
and skull shards scattered
on the groun

a formic feast
this pink-white shine
his white-pink slime
food for their journey home

in freeze-frame time
I declared you dead
as mama-san cried
her lonely tearful requiem

One night on a hill overlooking Plei Someplace
(2015/2019)

The rockets' red glare
and bombs bursting in air
are my anthem tonight
as I tune out my body
after a long and wearisome day as Medic
for these Base Camp commandos from 4th S&T,
secure in the knowledge that my rifle and my gun
are both close at hand
should either need arise.

If this had been theater
(at times it must have been)
Castanon, my Scrooge ghost at Fort Sam Houston,
would have shouted: "Break a leg!"
instead of defining my orders to the Nam
with his drunken morbid hex:

> *"You'll probably be one of the ones
> who comes back in a body bag
> with a tag on your toe, mi amigo!"*

In a dream more real than the present reality of the Nam,
I feel the coldness of Death's horrid breath on my face:

> mind's eye wide open in dreaming
> sees the dark soul of the people
> in black pajamas
> as I detect the pressure
> of a heavy weight on my chest.
> I feel the slicing of a knife across my throat
> and I sense that I'm being swept
> by the swift scythe of Death.

My physical eyes wide open, I rise from my dreaming
to see bright green tracers streaming from the valley below
and tearing through the darkly clouded sky
as they pass over the protective perimeter walls
that surround the village of Plei Someplace.

Body count
(1973)

unlaced,
his boot lies there —
no longer worn

in motionless existence
gaping
open-mouthed

its tongue is torn
and bloodied
by the mangled flesh within

as empty eyelets
gaze upon
the unmoving
silent form
that for a short time walked
the Central Highland foothills

a moist shadow of life
spilled on his spit and polish
dries darkly

There he lies
dust to dust

more earth now than man
he dreams of falling

never stopping
or wanting to

Dr. Dew explains his FUO diagnosis while the Mad Medic snickers
(1973)

So, it's not malaria, my friend.
Our days may be numbered, but you're not at your end.
You have a high fever and chills,
but if you took your pills
as instructed by your medic out in the field,
you could snooze all covered in blankets of *Anopheles;*
if you please, this seems hilarious—
they could drain you dry and you would die
from loss of blood, but no malarias.

We'll diagnose you with an FUO
(you must pronounce each letter separately, please).
Do not confuse this with a UFO;
we are the true aliens in the world of the Vietnamese.

It's called a Fever of Unknown Origin;
as you've seen, we doctors really do not know it all.
You'll get to rest in style in our medical ward while
we feed you some pills for the fever and chills,
and also those fabulous meals
from our first class mess hall—
but that's not all.

You'll need to drink a lot of water
(hydration is always the key)
so you can return to your regular duty,
much sooner than later
and you can fight in this god damn war again.
No, it's not malaria, my friend.

Ralpha
(1970)

Rolling over,
furry fluff-ball,
legs a-twitching to the tickle
of a friendly hand –
wet-tongued,
licking chicken off my fingers, Dog.

Chasing after
worn-out soldiers;
hind end swinging with the wagging
of her happy tail,
cold-nosed
wartime base camp comrade, Dog.

Raise a pup,
name her:
Laugh! We are children once again,
rolling over in the sparse grass.
Come and get me, fluff-bitch!
Rolling over, and over
and over.

While the war
goes on
somewhere else
beyond this happiness,
she barks
and makes us smile.

To a hamburger, while in the 'Nam
(1972/2018)

sometimes, I sense this taste in my mind
for an honest to goodness real
hamburger

the bun
lightly greased and toasted on the grill

fresh garden tomato
and pickle chips the flavor of dill

with mustard and mayo
a thick slice of sweet Texas onion

and table-shared:
a mountain of fries
with a light outer crunch; evenly golden

tea too: ice cold
and sweet, with a garnish of lemon

Orange Pekoe, to wash this well-formed
for my hands sandwich down
my esophagus

a distant memory
of lunch at the Cozy Café
on U.S. Highway 90, Flatonia, Texas

but here I get roast beast with greased gravy,
potatoes mashed, not the fried variety

with green beans, canned and
faded dull like the army fatigues we wear

tea too: instant and sweet
flavored with a squirt from a plastic lemon
mother sent from *"over there"*

Watchtower One on the perimeter of An Khe Base Hospital
(1970/2018)

Bicept clouds flext away their misty perspirations
most energetically on this hazy night of war.
Growling, grasping, powerful towers of fluff and circumstance
tossed around their flashing balls of lightning
across the night sky.
I was watching from my watchtower
at the foot of Hon Cong Mountain,
casting constant glances toward the grasses' sudden shiftings
as a breeze kissed off by muscled clouds
grazed their wavering tips.

An ER team lights up the "red crossed" helipad
for a groaning metal bird approaching.
As it veers to its left, passing behind my watchtower
the Huey's bright beam flashes dancing rainbows
through the slow precipitation.
Cutting through that heavy atmosphere,
the Medevac chopper's blades
slice through raindrops,
sluicing off each blade in turn
a lateral rain that splashes on my face.
     thump, thump
           thump, thump
                  thump…

I can see through the helicopter's open side door
a frantic medic CPR-ing
while a crewman's holding high a saline drip.
Their full attention is centered on a fair-haired soldier-boy
while behind them a lifeless body lies
zipped inside a body bag, another GI.
The young "Doc," with a determined expression

on his face, applies compression after compression
and each in their silent movement seems to intone:
"not this one, not this one, not this one."

thump, thump

thump, thump

thump...

Erection
(2015/2018)

Melodious mañanitas rising to the heavens:
a memory of awakening in Waelder, Texas,
to the early morning rustlings
of dull-feathered wrens.
Their songs echo in the upper corners
of Papa Grande's front porch
as they joyfully tell the world
that nest-making and mating begins.

Bird-like chirping at the entry to our hootch
wakes me from a restless morning sleep
after all-night duty, "Sergeant of the Guard."
From my bottom bunk, I look around and there
a-tittering, drab as wrens,
the laundry ladies who wash the dried out man stains
and the skid marks from our skivvies,
are bunched together.

Granny, with one hand shyly covering mouth,
is pointing with the other
at the bunk above me
where Little Dave is also resting
from his night-time guard task,
not all of him relaxed.

She's whispering to the youngest maid,
the one the soldiers all call *Baby-san*,
to look upon an American soldier's body part
blushing a blotchy rosy-pink, rigid at attention;
his covers are pushed down to his feet
due to his aroused heat.

Wrapping my sheet around me
I rise to shoo them, make them fly away.
Baby-san blushes; but Granny just giggles as
she wiggles a finger that moves up to her lips.
With a sly wink, she shushes me to not disturb
my bunkmate's dreaming.

Granny in An Khe
(2015)

Today, a drab green bird will come
to fly me away
to Cam Ranh Bay,
and I will soon be home.

In the haze of favored smokes the night before,
I bade farewell
to my "family" of brothers in the 'Nam –
the men who shared their stories
and at times laid bare their weaknesses.

Guess Who on the reel-to-reel was singing
"American Woman" in the background.
Once Canada beckoned and I said no,
and now this Canadian band
is calling me home.

On this last An Khe dawning
I need to find the time to say goodbye to Granny
and her sister laundry ladies
sitting Vietnamese style
in their morning circle
as they chatter away while scrubbing
off the dirt from the clothes of the friends
  I'll leave behind.

I join the ladies
eliciting giggles and blushes
as I squat down in their manner
to give thanks and say goodbye –
for forever.

Granny laughs and tells me: *"You are good man;*
you sit like Montagnard.
You be like us."
As she taps the "brownness" of my arm,
then that of her face, she says: *"same, same."*
I hug her close and we both cry a little.

Leader
(1970)

You cover your head now
in blanketed thoughts
of rainbow'd sunsets
after the deluge
has quenched a thirsty earth

I drink to you
ambrosia of the passing rain
from pools above the thunderheads

as clouds cast patterns
on the darkened hillsides
I watch the shadows from the moon

You wait a long while
for golden slumber to remove you
from the journey of the sun
to travel lightly
through your melancholy dreams

I followed in your steps
passing through the fallen arches
of your well-laid footprints

tripping on your shadow's shadow
the earth so soft to touch
the grass bends to my final breath…

A Colorado letter in parts, 2 Dec 70 / 9:20 PM (MST)
(1970/2020)

I don't save old shoes.
The worn out ones from high school graduation,
I don't know where they are.

When I came home *from the war,* mother
said my old shoes had been left at the old house,
but I didn't bother to go look for them.

They are of another life:
a good tale once lived, but now
we must lace new strings.

So when I hear of the old doors boarded up,
the windows now broken or pane-less,
and my outhouse reading room tipped over,

I sense that emptiness has now replaced
the ghosted brotherly good time laughter,
no longer adhering to the old house walls.

> *as if walls could laugh —*
> *or talk*
> *or even cry*

But even if my worn down shoes aren't found,
they could be memorialized, like baby shoes —
bronzed and shelved in a corner of the mind.

A Colorado letter in parts, 2 Dec 70 / 9:33 PM (MST)
(1970/2020)

You ask me, what good are memories?
Like a mental string around a finger,
they remind us of what was real.

They stimulate
the drying taste buds
of a worn-down mind.

When that plane left Cam Ranh Bay
everyone let out a yell of happiness —
but then came an empty silence.

And as I looked around, I could sense
that others left "brothers" behind
and they were trying to gather them

all into their hearts
for one last time before that strange
and screwed-up land below went out of view.

The one thing I did remember clearly
is that even though there were good times,
I was never sure I would live through it.

Last memory:
fishing boats
trawling in the South China Sea.

THE WALLET

by Cynthia Douglas-Ybarra

The wallet is thick and full, black and worn shiny from overuse, containing an undisclosed life. Stuck to the wall of the wallet, tucked in the very back corner, the corner that should have held frayed and wrinkled bills, dirty and worn, there with tattered edges from friction and undigested hope, was the green card. You could tell it had been there for some time, a quiet, smoldering ambition, a burning rebellion of sorts. "Fuck you, gringo, this is my green card."

His life was not reflected in the yellow caution signs greeting you as you get closer and closer to the border. Depictions of non-descript shadow families in silhouette dotting the San Ysidro port of entry, where 20,000 people, coming to clean shit off of porcelain thrones, raise verdant bits of fertile earth, or work in offices and shipyards cross northbound daily.

Wetback, beaner, spic, this litany of insults, like devotion, so easily brought forth from unyielding mouths. This is what I heard about my father as I was growing up. And because I am undeniably an extension, those words affected me too. What I can tell you about my father is that he spent his lifetime defending the country that spit contempt back into his face, telling him, in no uncertain terms, that he was beneath consideration. This man who had crossed meridians, shook Neptune's hand; this was a different kind of line crossing. Brown skin was the measure of his worth.

Pocha, not Mexican enough, not American enough. Denied a mother tongue by a father who knew, intimately, the burden of race, even though Latino is not considered a race, per se. The heavy load of always trying to prove yourself. Regardless of context, you have to do it 200% better.

The language is easy to understand, but by the time she puts the English into the Spanish, the conversation is long over. She is left standing with one foot firmly in the United States, the other tentatively planted in Mexico. White Latina? Is there such a thing? Is this a paradox, or was she faking it? How do you fake the blood coursing through your veins, this history of revolutionary grandmother, flags aloft, as she is honored at her wake? How do you fake family whose language is unlike yours, but their embrace feels like home while they teach you how to make tamales every Christmas Eve? What is the measure of enough? Who gets to decide? No soy suficiente? No soy lo suficientemente Latina?

The desert is a trickster, this biome of dehydration, the coyote, Huehuecóyotl, dualistic master of good and evil. Two hundred and thirty-two souls given over to the sand and sun, at the beginning of 2017. A consecrated sacrifice to the invisible border, demarcation between the worthy and those who are ineligible. How many more? Remnants of life and death preserved in a milk crate, skull stained red from bandana. A baseball, green ribbon, crucifix, a child's drawing, stuffed animal, psalms and revelations torn from the holy word, maybe as a last comfort, maybe a whispered plea for rescue that would never come.

Code 500, announcing the finding of flesh and bone. Desiccated tissue, blowflies, putrefaction, and maggot mass. The desert eats its dead fast. But when interrupted, bones and bodies are dropped into mass graves, thrown easily, like thoughtlessly tossed garbage on a city street. Never given a second thought. Manifest destiny culminated into diaspora, murder and war. December 30th is a day of mourning for some. California, New Mexico, Arizona, Utah, Colorado and Nevada, spoils of the Mexican-American war. Why do they try to cross back into what was once theirs? Those red *Make America Great Again* hats should factually read *Make America Mexico Again.* America is a continent, divided by man-made borders. "Fuck you gringo, this is my green card." The color of your skin is the measure of your worth.

Slogans of empty and misguided bitterness; *build the wall, go back where you belong, America, love it or leave it,* slip so easily from the mouths of colonizers. Who are they keeping out? Or is it about keeping somebody in? Will it come down to the seizure or division of over 5000 privately owned and tended properties along the U.S. Mexican border? This is just one of its costs.

Vigilantes, military wannabes, in desert camo and boonie hats. NVGs, Ar-15s and other weaponry and military like gadgets line their trucks, decorative testicles hanging off of the towing ball mounts swaying in the rhythm with the occasional gust of dust and wind. These are men on a mission. They patrol in the sun and at dusk, full water bottles; beer bellies hanging over belted cammo, hunting for illegals, illegitimate, felonious, brown humans who would dare cross over into the land belonging to their ancestors. This is vacation for some of them. While wives and children frolic in warm pacific waters, in the land known as Mexico, they live out the fantasy that one day they will bring down that cartel and all the bad hombres with it. These men will tell you that they are on assignment from God and like those who came before them, see this as a moral undertaking, their duty to country and fellow men. Manifest destiny, continentalism-giving way to colonialism. "Fuck you Gringo, this is my green card."

If you had a chance to ask him where he was from, my father would proudly state San Jose, California, though San Nicolas de Ibarra, Jalisco Mexico is his real home. His father was from Jalisco, his mother from Spain. He concealed his true name, and by default, mine. He chopped it up and turned it into something alien and unintelligible. This denies his roots and heritage. It was akin to sweeping the memory of his rolled r's, his indiscernible accent under the rug.

His skin, though, tells another story. You can't wash away the brown. There is truth to the saying, "If you're black get back, if your brown, stick around, if you're white, you're all right." Skin color, in its various tones, is destiny. DNA, double helixes, lettered pairs, ATCG, we are all made of alphabet packages. This means nothing. It does not bring the barriers down, does not create understanding or bridges that close gaps that exist between. Yet the same blood courses through all of us. It is red, replete with hemoglobin, deliverer of life, and it flows through all who possess backbone. And if we lose enough of it, we die. Is it not enough that we bleed the same blood?

The wallet is thick and full, black and worn shiny from overuse, containing an undisclosed life.

THE STORY OF ME

Joe Vaverka a.k.a. Joseph Caverns (Spellchecker for "Vaverka"= "Caverns")

(Editor's note: Upon the request of the author, the following was not edited)

70 years ago I almost died for the first time, a purple baby. Lucky for me there were no purple people eaters for another 8 years. Dad gave me a transfusion and off I went. I had a void in my throat and didn't talk much I was in my own world. My fourth grade teacher tried to get us to read House of seven gables and Little Woman and tell her the deep thoughts of the stories. I liked Mad Magazine. She is probably laughing hysterically looking down at me writing stories. I kept flunking English but got B's in physics. Everybody tried to teach me to type with 10 fingers, I still type with 2, 4 if my Parkinson's is not showing. In my 20s I found Syfy and mystery's. 1980 I did 3 how to articles on fiberglass repair for the National Corvette Restorers Society Published all 50 states and 19 country's. About 2002 or 3 the VA screwed up my meds and wiped out the 80's & 90's and fast recall. Ough It'll all come back It didn't. I started reading and journaling as much of my past as I could remember to wake up my brain. Rereading it later jogged a memory, I wrote that down or rather typed it into the computer. On rare days can I read my writing. I started writing the story's of our weekend trips and finally did a fiction. It just flowed out. My best ideas came at 3 or 4 in the morning I kept a note pad in the bathroom and hoped I could figure it out in the morning. Some stories come all at once 6 Hours and I'm done. Some come in spurts like One Boat - Two People 10 point 17 pages an action adventure love story. The movie The Expendables made love with the Hallmark channel. I try to stick with comedy. My Star Trek 27th century is very much different from Kirk's 24th. Mine has 300 year old beautiful female doctors in robot bodies and

a Bigfoot as security chef named Rabbi Ezra Ben Lipschitz. My Bert Cat and Jack stories has Bigfoot's Jackalops and in one chapter they went to Romania to visit Doctor Frankenstein DDS to help find his old monster who is lost. When the world gets over whelming I go write a story. I was going to try and get self published this year but not with the economy in the toilet.

MURDER IN D MAJOR AND D MINOR (TWO SHARPS AND A FLAT)

by John Achor

Rhonda McQuaid's mind could only process one concept—I've got to get out of this town.

Saturday night and she finished the second set at Scooters, a smallish bar across county line from the only city for miles. She eased her Les Paul Gibson electric guitar onto the vertical stand and stepped down from the stage. Elbowing past Sam Barstow, she moved to the small table reserved for performers. Ted Carsten, the bartender, put a paper napkin on the table and placed a draft beer in front of her. "Rhonda, hope Sam's not going to hassle you."

"Sam can't get it through his thick head we're history."

Ted assumed his old hang dog expression. "Well, if there's anything I can do for you…"

"You're a dear, Ted," Rhonda said. "I'll yell if I need help, and please ask Gretchen to put another bottle of water on the stage for me."

Looking up, she said, "Sam Barstow, there's nothing left for us to say. Please don't sit down or cause a scene."

Sam spoke in a low growling tone and animated his speech with arm gestures. She glanced toward the bar and saw Ted and his assistant, Gretchen, both watching. Ted said something to Gretchen and walked away. Sam slumped into a chair, and she left him in the dark corner.

Several minutes later, Sheriff Buster Richfield stepped onto the platform, interrupted the music and bellowed. "Anyone know who the Ford F-150 with the fancy paint job belongs to?"

Rhonda leaned over and said, "Sam. Sam Barstow owns that truck." The sheriff took Rhonda by the arm and produced handcuffs. "Well, ol' Sam's truck has a flat tire, and he's layin' next to it a chewin' up gravel with a stab wound in his chest.

"What's that got to do with me?" Rhonda said.

"I heard him and you got into it here tonight. I think you mighta had something to do with his killin'."

Several people shouted an alibi for Rhonda saying she was on stage before Sam walked out of Scooters. Buster relented, let go of her arm and in his most authoritative voice, said, "Don't leave town."

The crowd melted away. Rhonda slipped her guitar into the soft fabric case and returned it to its stand. She turned to see her, on again-off again boyfriend, Chet Longstreet grinning at her. "C'mon, darlin' let's blow this joint."

"Oh, Chet. You always know how to sweet talk a gal." Her sarcasm was lost on the hulking hunk in cowboy clothing. She liked him, but he was missing a lug nut or two in the culture department.

Ted Carsten came out from behind the bar. "Sorry for all the trouble, Rhonda, let me know if there's anything I can do to help."

"Keep your nose out of our business," Chet said.

Rhonda jerked her arm from Chet's grip. "Don't be making decisions for us. I can take care of my own world." Chet got his "hurt" look, stopped but said nothing. Rhonda left him standing with his mouth open.

In the parking lot, Rhonda saw Sam Barstow still lying on his back in the gravel. There was a large stain next to him where he bled out. The truck was in the aisle leading out of the parking lot. She surmised Sam got into his truck without seeing the flat, then noticed the flat dragging, got out and someone caught him there.

Rhonda walked toward her car and smiled at Sheriff Buster. He repeated his earlier warning "Don't leave town." She gunned out of the parking lot. In the rear-view mirror, she saw Chet standing in the trail of dust billowing behind her.

* * *

A week later, Rhonda was back at Scooters. She still carried an image in her mind of Sam Barstow lying in the gravel.

Sheriff Buster strode close to the stage. He got Rhonda's attention and pointed to his eyes with two fingers. Rhonda figured it was a signal telling her he was keeping an eye on her, but said "Buster, if you're trying to pick your nose, you missed." He turned and stalked to the bar.

Chet Longstreet was standing in front of the stage staring at her. "Rhonda, how come you ain't paying me no mind this week?"

"I spent the week trying to figure out who killed Sam. I didn't have much time for dating."

"That's all well an' good," he said, "but I'm gettin' pretty horny sittin' around waitin' for you."

"Don't be melodramatic, Chet." She looked over his shoulder and saw Ted standing behind him. Ted had a bottle of water and his foot pawed the floor like a horse counting out the answer to a math problem. "Ted, come on up here with that water. Nobody's going to bite you."

Chet made a lunging motion, but pulled up short. Ted flinched, then placed the water on the table. Chet stared at him the entire time, and Ted retreated to the bar.

The members of the group assembled on the stage and began the evening's entertainment. Rhonda flailed at the steel strings of the Gibson without enthusiasm. She kept thinking of Sam's death. The fact that Chet glared at her from his seat, never looking away, unnerved her. Near the end of the first set, Rhonda's pick flipped out of her fingers and disappeared behind the stage. She borrowed one from the other guitarist, but it wasn't the same. At intermission, she told the group she would be back shortly.

She walked toward the front door and saw Chet get up and follow her. Outside she wheeled and confronted him. "I don't need you traipsing after me."

It brought Chet up short. "Damnit, Rhonda. If you don't pay me more notice, I'll..."

She ignored him, got the spare picks from the glove box in her wagon and headed back inside. She left Chet, hands on hips, standing in the middle of the parking lot doing his best to stare holes through her.

* * *

Playing again, Rhonda was glad she took the time to get her extra picks and the chords came easier as her pick danced over the steel strings. She was relaxed and having fun.

Buster came huffing across the dance floor and leaped onto the stage. He grabbed the microphone and shouted, "Don't nobody leave this here place. We got us another murder out in the parkin' lot."

"Who the hell is it this time, Sheriff?" someone shouted.

"Chet Longstreet's done been stabbed in the chest. Just like Sam Barstow." He turned to Rhonda. "An' this time, little Missy, you ain't got no alibi. I seen him and you go out the front door together. You come back in, but Chet didn't. I went out there and he was, dead."

The sheriff dragged Rhonda off to jail, but soon realized he had no direct evidence linking her to the killing. He let her go, "for now," adding the same old warning about leaving town.

* * *

Another week. Another Saturday night. Two men dead and Sheriff Buster didn't have a clue. The band was nearing the end of the last set. Ted slipped to the side of the platform and handed Rhonda a new bottle of water. She nodded a thank you to him and unscrewed the cap. It came off easier than usual. A couple of swigs and she was back into the music.

Tonight, Rhonda decided to take her guitar home with her, so when the music ended, she slipped it into the soft case and started for her station wagon. Reaching the car, she pulled the back door down and slid the guitar inside. She turned and was surprised to see Ted.

"How's the water taste?" he said.

She took another swig and thought about the loosened cap. She looked at Ted, then at the water bottle and realized something was wrong. "How did you get out here so fast?"

Ted grinned. "There's a trapdoor behind the bar and I can slip out the cellar's storm door. That's how I got out here the last two Saturday nights without being seen." His grin turned to a frown. "Rhonda, I've done so much for you. Will you marry me?"

Her head felt light and her knees were turning to rubber. "Marry you? We don't even date—how can I marry you?"

"If I can't have you, nobody will!"

She saw the knife in his hand as he advanced. What the hell can I do? By now, Ted was about five feet from her. She leaned back and sat on the lip of the wagon's storage area. Her hand groped behind her and found the neck of the guitar. Rhonda pushed herself to a standing position dragging the Gibson behind her. She brought it up, took a two-hand grip on the neck and swung. The guitar body caught Ted flush on the side of his head with the crunch of breaking wood and the twang of steel strings.

Rhonda slumped to the ground. Blackness receded, the world came back into focus, and she saw Sheriff Buster Richfield waving a hand in front of her face. The ammonia from the capsule jarred her awake.

Buster said, "Well, little lady, I guess you solved the killin's. That knife ol' Ted was a carryin' shore does look like it could be the murder weapon."

Rhonda nodded a weak smile. It's time to shake the dust of this place off my boots. Her mind was already planning the route she would take to get away.

THE STORM, THE DEMONS, AND LOVE

by Donald Dingman

The storm's whistling grew louder as it approached and ended with a crash of thunder. Its wind, breaking windows and blowing loose items like tumbleweeds. The wail of the sirens scant minutes before the storm hit the area saved everyone who wasn't already sheltered. Bill Hornaday was one of the transients who made it to the homeless shelter before the storm hit the old abandoned factory building he and the others called home.

Bill flipped up his collar and pulled his ball cap down, preparing to exit the shelter and head back to his home. *Home,* he thought as he entered the light rain after the storm. *A funny thing to call a clear space on an old factory building floor. I sure wish I could go back to my real home.*

He was the first man back to the storm ravaged building. Some of his old friends were down getting a five finger discount; others stayed in the shelter. All alone, he learned against the wall, staring at the shards of broken glass that sparkled from the rays of the morning sun, "Looks like diamonds all over the floor. Too bad they aren't real. Then again, what good would pockets full of diamonds do me? I'd be accused of stealing them and locked up." He pushed off the wall to begin his search for the items he had hurriedly left behind before the storm claimed the space.

Other than the glass, the floor appeared to have been power washed with everything pushed to the furthest wall and left to rot. It took him an hour to find his duffle bag and case of pictures buried under the rubble in the corner of an old room, still dry. "I guess the wind got her first. Thank God." He brushed the dirt off the case and opened it. All of his family pictures were dry inside. He closed and held it close, thanking God that not all was lost.

Scanning the floor for any other usable items, he saw a body laying like it had been tossed aside. Bill shivered as he stared at the body, obviously not alive. He closed his eyes and his tears preceded the images of all of the men he had killed, and the ones he couldn't save, in individual vignettes. He counted the six he had killed, and four of his brothers he couldn't save. Two of them were next to him when they died. His anger came quickly, and he found himself pounding his fists against his duffle bag.

"Thank God. I never did that to my family," he told himself after taking out the anger on his bag. He wiped his eyes and opened the case of pictures. Finding the one of his wife, he sat against a wall and talked to it. "I never wanted to hurt you or the kids. I couldn't trust myself. I'm sorry I ran away." He raised his head, "Please, God, help her to understand my problems."

He went to the body and rolled it over. It was a mannequin from a store, still dressed. Relieved, he moved on to find another spot to set up home for the night. He walked the floor and up to the next. Finding it cleaner, he set himself behind an interior wall for protection from the wind. Moving a couple of items of junk, he found a stack of six clean white leather bound books tied with a string.

Sitting down, he picked up the top one, thumbing through the pages. They were all blank, as was the rest of the books. *Hmm. Maybe I should start a diary of my exploits for my family after I'm dead,* he thought, putting them into his bag.

Later, after going to the shelter for a bowl of soup, he returned to the rubble of his self- imposed isolation. He gathered some dry debris and made a small warming fire. Throughout the day, he was joined by a few of the other "tenants" of the building to share his fire for warmth and conversation. Several talked with him about their experiences in their respective wars. Those conversations almost always ended in tears for both them and Bill.

Late in the afternoon, the sound of his name being called made Bill look up to see a cleanly dressed friend from the VA center classes he had attended, but never stuck out to the finish. The friend said, "You should go down to the shelter. More storms are forecast for tonight. I'm going around to pass the word. Will you be going?"

Bill smiled and looked around the empty floor. "I'm not sure. Surviving that last storm took me back to the war. You know, being hunkered down in a tight group and no way to defend yourself. I'm afraid that I'd do something crazy if I was in the shelter again like that. Last night was really rough on me. I'll just stay here. Thanks for the invitation, though."

"Okay. Nobody's forcing you. Remember where to go if it gets too bad. I'll check back in a couple of days."

"Thanks, I'll be fine," he said, shaking the man's hand before he departed.

Bill opened the first book and began thinking on where he should start his diary. He took out a few pictures of his buddies from the war. That is when he decided to start writing about the demons that sent him from home. He sat and began thinking on what he was going to write, letting the fire burn itself out before he retired for the night, wrapped in his wool army blanket. It was the only thing along with a few clothes in his duffle bag he had taken with him when he left home. His old uniform and such, he left in a footlocker back at home. After waking the next morning, he made his bathroom call in the portable outhouse a construction crew had left behind, but somehow still maintained.

Making sure all of the pictures were in the case and the new books in his duffle, Bill headed out to find a new home. He found his new domicile, an actual office in another abandoned building, complete with a desk and a chair. "Ah, at least I can sit off the floor while I write in the books." He set his bag on the desk and checked out the room. During his search, he found a key on the floor that worked the door lock. "Wow, I can't believe it. My own room with a locking door. This must be my lucky day," he said, wiping the surface of the desk and the chair with his coat sleeve before sitting and pulling out a blank book.

Having the urge to give his mental demons a life on paper, he started writing. He lost track of time until his stomach growled. "Okay, fellas, we'll go get you some food," he told his belly before scanning what he had written. He read about the first four men he had killed and the circumstances of each. Seeing them writ-ten down, somehow made it easier to see how menacing they were, trapped in his subconscious. "Perhaps those classes really did me some good." He noticed that his memories filled over half way through the first book and chuckled. "My diary of the men I have killed." That would be the perfect title to this book."

It was still light outside when he locked his new home, heading for his eve-ning meal. The owner of a fancy Italian restaurant, a veteran himself, had an alcove setup in the alley behind his restaurant for homeless vets. He served only an evening meal, but he was rewarded with praise from those who patronized it, who took it upon themselves to keep the place well cleaned, making sure the health department didn't shut the place down. Bill ate a meal of spaghetti with marinara sauce, a bread stick, along with a small glass of wine for which he spent his last dollar.

Back at his desk, Bill caressed the white leather cover before opening it to read what he had written. The blank pages he had not touched were now filled with handwriting that wasn't his, but the words were just what he would have written. They were his feelings for sure. It covered the last two men he had killed before going right into his feelings on the men he couldn't save.

He picked up a second book. It too was filled with words in the same handwriting. It was the story of his life beginning with his birth. Every page described a day in his life. He flipped the pages back and forth, unbelieving that all of his life was able to be written into a book. It skipped to the last page. It read the date of his tenth birthday. He grabbed the next book; it ended with his twentieth birthday and so on until he found the last book. It was blank except for his pictures inserted between the pages.

"The last book with the photos is the one that is most important," came a lyrical female voice. Bill looked up to see a lovely dark haired woman in a long white robe, standing by the desk. She remained there even after he rubbed his disbelieving eyes.

"I must be dead. St. Peter came and wrote my life down so I could see where I strayed, showing how I made my path down to Hell." He looked at the photos slowly, one by one, before looking up to the woman. "Okay. You can now send me down there. I'm ready."

She sat with one leg on the desk, hands in her lap, facing him, and said, "I'm not here to send you to Hell. I'm not here to take you up to Heaven, either. That last book is not blank. It is full of the worries, wonders, and questions of the people in those pictures on why you left them. You need to answer them. Your family is thinking that they should start considering applying for death benefits for your wife. It has been the legal seven years. She is still holding out hope."

She handed him a small notebook, and address book, by the writing on the cover. "You need to start reconnecting with them. Your wife still doesn't understand why you left. Go to her and tell her about your demons. She'll understand. She still loves you and wants to help." With those words, she put her hand on his shoulder.

He closed his eyes in sleep and dreamed of his family and the good times they had before the demons reared their heads. In another dream, he read the questions from the book out to the gathered family, answering each one as he read it.

It was nearing sunset when Bill's eyes opened. He only vaguely remembered any dreams. He felt it was time to go home, *now*. Not tomorrow. He gathered the books and the picture case into the duffle bag, threw it over his shoulder, and locked his new home's door. "Just in case," he told himself.

It was only a block from his start when he heard a scream and stopped, focusing his ear for another one. When it came, he realized it was a young girl's scream, full of fear for her life.

The screams grew softer in volume as he ran toward them, knowing he to hurry to save her because she was either close to death or she was being gagged.

At the alley entrance, he saw a female teenager fighting off three men. He admired her ability despite the odds she was facing. Obviously, the three young men weren't homeless and wanted her for her body, live or dead. A scene from the war came to his mind. One that he hadn't helped a girl and she was killed. *Not this time* he thought as he dropped his bag and charged into battle.

Bill tackled the two men holding her legs, allowing her freedom to fight for her life with the man with the knife. They were young enough to get up quickly, but Bill's experience gave him the edge to grab their shoulders and slam their heads together. Letting them drop, he turned his focus on the third man, holding onto the girl with a knife against her neck. "You best be letting her go or you will end up like those other two," he told him.

The young man tightened his grip. "Leave us, old man or I will do her, then you. Those two are just young punks. They don't have the guts to actually kill her. I do."

"Well son, maybe you do. Maybe it is only talk to boost your bravado. I don't have to brag. I have the medal for killing six enemy soldiers by hand in combat. They were a lot tougher than you."

"Yeah, so? That was so long ago, old man. You couldn't whip a puppy now."

"Smart boy. Do you think I was lucky with those two dead boys over there? Go ahead, slowly move over there and see if I'm lying. They aren't just sleeping. Just don't cut that girl or you will join them."

The man walked the girl over to the bodies. Looking down, he saw Bill was right and turned back to the homeless man. "So you managed to kill them. But I've got the girl. You won't do anything to hurt her in the process of getting to me."

Bill made a gesture, twisting his hand. "That's true, but have you forgotten that the girl might have the balls to come up with a twist to get away on her own?"

"She's too scared to think right now," the man said right before the girl grinned at Bill, signally receipt of the message, before grabbing her captor's testicles with a hard twist. He let her loose and was cold cocked by her right fist. He went down hard and didn't move.

Bill saw the small pool of blood coming from the man's head before grabbing the girl to keep her from staring at the man. He knew the feeling all too well. He grabbed her to stifle her scream into his coat. "Shh. Yes. He is dead. You did it in self-defense." He comforted her as she sobbed while he scanned the alley for signs of cameras. Not seeing any, he whispered a silent thank you to the air. He thought back to the woman in the office. *She had to be an angel. She knew I wouldn't be waiting until tomorrow. I was supposed to be here in this alley.*

The girl looked up at Bill, studying his bearded face. "Thank you. I never could have lasted to take care of all of them."

"I'm glad you caught my reference to his supposed manhood. I wasn't expecting the punch to his eye, though. That was a good one. Are you okay, otherwise?"

After releasing her, she checked herself over and nodded that she was. "Is he really dead?"

"Yes. Now we should get out of here before the cops come and find us with three dead guys laying at our feet."

She looked at him, turning her head in different ways before she said, "You look familiar. Have we met before?"

"Only if you come around this part of town. I don't leave it much anymore."

She dusted off her clothes and gave him another look before they began looking for her purse and phone.

"I believe this one is yours?" he asked.

"Yes, thank you. I just found my purse. I guess I better get back home. Mom is going to kill me if I don't get home by midnight."

Bill glanced at her phone, seeing her name. He smiled, thinking how the angel had told him his family was still worried about him. Now, he saw that she was right. He hadn't recognized his granddaughter. The only photo of her was one from ten years ago. He handed the phone to her, holding her hand in his. "What brings a pretty young woman, like you, to come down to this part of town? Are you looking to get killed? Those three guys would have gladly obliged your wishes." He smiled. "No, I think you are in search of a lost family member to take him back into the family fold. Am I right?"

She looked at him again. "Yes, it is my grandfather I'm looking for. Maybe you know him. His name his Bill Hornaday."

"I know exactly where he lives. I'll escort you. That way nobody else will bother you." He stared at the girl for a moment, grinned, and put his arm around her shoulder. "Well, Belinda, I really think we should leave here now. I'm sure your mother would freak out when the cops call and say you were arrested for murdering three men."

"Did I really kill that guy?"

"Yes. I was the only witness. I looked. There are no cameras in the alley. Now please forget this alley and all that happened here. It will ruin your mind for love and send you down the wrong path, like me."

It took her a moment to realize that he called her by name. "How do you know my name and how my mother would react?" she asked.

He chuckled, "I read it on your phone. All mothers are the same."

Bill picked up his duffel and Belinda noticed the name stenciled on it. "Grandpa? Is that really you?"

"How did you guess?"

"Your bag has your name on it. You looked familiar. I just don't remember you ever having a beard." She held his arms and stared into his face. "It is you. You always had a glint in your eyes whenever I visited you and Grandma. Even when I was almost in junior high. Didn't you recognize me?"

Bill sat down in a doorway alcove. "Not until I read your name on your phone." He opened his bag and saw that only one book, not six were in it. "Where are they? Nobody was around when I dropped it to help you in the alley."

"What are you looking for?"

"Books. I had six books in here. My whole life story. Now there is only one." He slumped back against the door frame. "I guess the angel was wrong. She told me that the last one was full of questions of the people that loved and missed me. Now that I have killed again, that is all to waste." As soon as the words were out of his mouth, he began sobbing.

Belinda sat next to him and stroked his upper arm. Soothingly, she said, "I think I understand. At least you can know that I really appreciate the help back there. I much rather be sitting here comforting you than being back there bleeding all over the place."

"Thank you," he sobbed as she put her arm around his shoulder. After he finish crying, he wiped his eyes on his sleeves and opened the case and handed it to her. These are the pictures that have kept me going these years. Take a picture of me so they know I am not dead, then take them home. I've killed again. I can't go back now. I don't trust myself."

Belinda sat next to him, looking at the pictures in the case. She let him calm down before she stood up and put her fists on her hips. "Grandpa! You are coming home with me. I understand how you feel. I have joined your demon club, remember? Are you going to come willingly? Or am I going to have to take you down an alley and give you the whoopin' that you deserve for running out on Grandma?"

"Why should you care if I die alone out here?"

"I care. Mom cares, and so does Grandma. She is worried sick. You have no idea how hard it is to hear her praying constantly for your soul and safe return to her. She's lost weight and can even fit into my clothes. That is not right for a woman her age. Don't you care for her? You made a vow a long time ago to love, honor, and cherish. I've heard that tape of the ceremony that she plays so much, I can recite it word for word. Now get up and let's go."

Bill looked up with his red eyes. "I told you I can't now. I'll escort you to your car or however you got here and then you get your rear home." He noticed that her face was getting angry at him. He knew he should go, but the fear was holding him back.

Bill blinked his eyes and saw the angel standing beside his granddaughter who told him, "Go with her, Bill. She is the answer to the prayer you made down in the shelter the other night."

"Grandpa. What's wrong? You look like you've seen a ghost," Belinda asked when she saw the color drain from his face.

Feeling a hand on her shoulder, Belinda turned to see the angel. "He's okay. It's just the shock of seeing his prayers being answered." The angel caught Belinda before she collapsed in a faint and sat her down next to Bill, waiting until they were cognizant before vanishing.

"Did you see an angel?" Belinda asked.

"Yes. She's the same one who told me to go home tomorrow. Well, actually she said I needed to start reconnecting with family. Did you see her too?"

"She told me that you were in shock from seeing your prayer answered. I fainted after that. I just woke up sitting next to you. So you think she is still here?"

They both smiled, knowing she was.

"How are we getting home?"

"I parked my car in an attended lot a few blocks from here. I've seen those movies where girls get kidnapped in those underground garages." Belinda hugged him. "I love you, Grandpa. Thanks for being alive and for helping me back there."

She sniffed the air. "No kisses before you get cleaned up. You stink."

"I can only imagine your mother's face when we show up." He gathered the one book and the photo case into his bag. "Let's go before the angels get tired of me."

Belinda pulled out her phone and called her mother. "Mom. I'm going to be a little late. I met a friend and we started talking and lost track of time. I love you. Bye."

They were laughing and talking as they neared the alley where they found each other when they saw the flashing lights of police cars. They quickened their pace to clear the entry before an of the cops noticed them. A short distance passed the alley, Bill asked, "I wonder what happened back there."

"I guess three gang-bangers got their comeuppance. No innocent victims involved. Don't worry about it. That alley doesn't have surveillance cameras."

Bill laughed and squeezed her arm tighter. "Perfect answer, killer. I won't lose any sleep over it if you won't."

"Deal. Now we need to come up with a story that Grandma and Mom will believe about how I found you. I could tell them the truth, but it would sound so farfetched, they wouldn't believe it."

"Why not? I can verify that you are lying to protect your ass. I"ll tell them the truth. You met someone who knew me. He escorted you to me. That's the truth. They don't need to know that I was that someone."

Belinda looked up at her ragged bearded grandfather and smiled. "I like your truth better."

After they were on the road in the car, Belinda looked over at him. "Grandpa. Don't worry about those demons. You left them back there in that alley. You acted out of love for your fellow man. Once you wrote about them, they left your heart. Now they will only be a bad memory."

"How did you get so smart?"

"I had a mother who listened to her father. She taught me. Well, I guess she didn't teach me how to whoop ass. Must be in the genes I got from my grandfather. He was a decorated soldier."

"Sounds like he was a good man."

"Still is. He had some mental issues from the war. Now he is better. I sure hope he talks about those demons. I killed a man tonight, and I want to know how he coped with it."

"I told you to forget that alley."

"I can't. Just like you can't forget those men. It's a burden, but one I now share with you. We'll beat this thing together. You, me, and Grandma."

"Are you going to leave your parents in the dark?"

She laughed. "What happened in that alley stays in the alley. We are out of the Twilight Zone and heading home."

"Thank God for angels and granddaughters. Can you call your grandma while driving? I'd like to hear her voice before we meet."

Belinda made a couple of taps on the screen, handed it to him to hear, "Belinda, honey. What's up with my favorite grandchild?"

"Hi, Rachael. Belinda did what no one else could do. She found me and is bringing me home."

"Bill?"

"Yes. I am alive and well. Call Bonnie." He looked over to his granddaughter. "We are going to have a family reunion. Run me a bath. My little Belle says I stink. I can't wait to see you."

They talked a few minutes before hanging up. He turned to Belinda. "Well, my partner in crime. We did it."

Belinda put her hand on his. "We sure did. I love you, Grandpa."

"I love you too. Call me Bill. You've earned the right."

She giggled. "Bill, do we have enough time to stop for a chocolate ice cream cone at the drive in? It's been so long since you've taken me there."

"Well, my young whippersnapper. I don't have any money on me right now. But if you do, I'll consider it a pleasure to be treated by you."

"Just what I was hoping you'd say. Two large cones coming up."

The two walked into Bill's house where he was assaulted with kisses from his wife. After several, she noticed both of their attire. "Did you get into a street fight? I've never seen our little Belinda in such a condition. Or did you put up such a fight that she had to take you down a notch or two?"

"Grandma, Bill helped me out of a jam with three boys. We left them sleeping in some deserted alley." She turned to Bill, "Now you go get cleaned up. I'll wash up in the other bathroom."

"Welcome home, my love."

Bill wrapped his arms around her, giving her a kiss. "Thank you for not giving up on me."

"Never. I knew you would come home. My prayers were answered tonight."

Belinda laughed softly as she watched her grandparents head to the bathroom, arms wrapped around each other. "So were ours."

GIFTS

by Jen Stastny

On July 3, 2014, just after 8:00 a.m. London time, I bought a pair of fuchsia running shoes from a store near Parliament. I had been traveling for over a week with my then-husband, Liam, in Paris and Marseille, and I finally conceded that, despite being a veteran traveler, I had, once again, brought the wrong shoes. Since I had to spend another month there studying Chaucer's *Canterbury Tales* at the University of London, I needed something better.

Wearing my new shoes out of the store, I led Liam over to Parliament, and I stood staring at the gargoyles, trying to memorize them for my dad. I took pictures, too, of course, but I needed to remember how it felt to stand there and see.

My parents had given my brother, sister, and me the gift of travel when we were young. They took us on two six-week road trips to the West and then East coasts when we were in elementary school. They taught us how to navigate, to explore, to value the open land and experiences. We were not wealthy people, which I always knew, but it wasn't until I was an adult that I fully realized how much our parents sacrificed to give us those gifts and others. The summer after my junior year in high school, they sent me to France for a month to improve my language and travel skills. I went as an exchange student to Russia for a month less than a year later. During my third year in college, I studied in Besançon, France, for a semester and backpacked around the British Isles. For those trips and every subsequent trip I took, my dad only asked that I tell him about what I saw. We would sit through the night and into the early morning, at the dining table, and I would just talk. He answered with, "Is that so?" or, "Curious." He showed his admiration with short phrases. By the time I was standing there in front of Parliament, marveling at the gargoyles climbing, frozen, down the building, I had been to sixteen countries and forty-seven U.S. states, and we had logged countless hours talking about it.

"What are you staring at?" Liam asked.

"I'm trying to remember it all so I can tell my dad." Pause. "Why couldn't we just bring him here? He would love this."

"Could he take the walking?"

"We'd have to use a wheelchair, but so? He has to have a good seven or eight years left, right? My grandma lived to be 88." At the time, my dad was 81.

From there, we headed to the underground station to a destination I no longer recall. As we entered the station, I received a text from my sister: "Call me."

I rushed to the street level for better reception. After the inhumanly long few rings, Laura answered. She explained that our dad had woken up at 2 a.m. having difficulty breathing and asked our mom for an ambulance. While he was dressing, his heart stopped. At the exact moments I was buying pink shoes, my dad was dying. The paramedics restarted his heart after more than thirty minutes of CPR, and while Laura and I were on the phone, our dad had not yet regained consciousness but was breathing against the respirator, a good sign.

"Don't come home yet," she said. "Dad'll kill us if he wakes up and finds out you came home."

Liam and I spent the day seeking Wi-Fi so we could have more consistent updates. One bookstore we tried was hosting Hillary Clinton for a book signing that day. My dad hated Hillary Clinton. I looked forward with maniacal glee to telling him I'd been in such close proximity to his "favorite" politician.

At approximately ten that night, fewer than fourteen hours after our dad had first collapsed, Laura called me to tell me to come home, that he had died.

We were home by 1 p.m. the following day due to a miraculous combination of time zones and very few English people wanting to fly to the U.S. on the Fourth of July. We celebrated the Fourth as a family because it was our dad's favorite holiday.

The following week flew and crept. As a family, we picked out a cemetery plot, a coffin, a head stone. We picked out music. We wrote eulogies.

At the visitation, women in their 80's, some who had known my dad since elementary school, approached me tentatively, placing veined, papery-skinned hands upon my shoulders, and said, "You're Rex's daughter. You look just like him."

"Yes," I replied as I thought, *What woman doesn't want to be told she looks just like her dad?*

"You have to go back to London," they all said. "That's what he would have wanted." One after another, they all said the same thing. They were in cahoots with my family.

On the eighth day since my dad had died, I flew alone back to London to study with teachers from all over the U.S. Grief threatened to capsize me; I'd never experienced that type of tired.

My amazing sister sent me on scavenger hunts each day after my classes, telling me to visit this park or that sculpture, and to send her selfies to prove I'd completed her tasks. My new friend Lori, from Rhode Island, generously accompanied me on these adventures. My Austrian friend, Julia, met me in Belgium for a long weekend. Slowly, travel began to heal me. By doing what my dad taught me to love, I found myself again, buried in all that sorrow.

I don't have any children of my own to inherit the gifts I've received from my father, but as a high school teacher, I use my knowledge of travel to help my students make their worlds as broad as possible. I'm lucky to be included in a group of teachers who travel with students to study history. In the U.S., we've visited New York City, Washington, D.C., Virginia, Alabama, and Louisiana. The summer after my dad died, we took our first group to Europe for two weeks.

The students were exemplary every day, but one day stands out in particular. The focus of our trip was World War II, so we were in Bastogne. We had a free hour for lunch in the town square, so I used the opportunity to take an introvert moment down a cobbled street, unpopulated by our students. Pounding footsteps and cries of, "Ms. Stastny! Ms. Stastny!" shattered my respite. "We need help!" they cried.

What they actually wanted was to order their sandwiches in the deli in French, and, since I speak French, they "needed" me. I stood at the front of the line next to the cash register and as the students pointed at what they wanted on the menu in my hand, I whispered in their ears the words they needed to say. My proper French pronunciation turned into something else entirely when uttered from their mouths, but my teacher ability to stage whisper allowed the cashier to understand what each student wanted.

As I ate my sandwich on the bus to our next destination, having had no quiet moment to myself, I thought about telling my dad about those kids and those sandwiches, and I heard him chuckling, smiling at me with his eyes cast down to the table, and saying, "Very good, Jennifer. Very good."

THROUGH MY TEAMMATE'S EYES

by Mary Baker

What do you see when I look at you, like you look at me?
Do you trust me enough to stay, or are you going to flee?
Is there peace in your eyes or piles of unrest?
Do you know how much I care, and want to pass your test?
What would you have me do? What would you like me to say?
Is there any way I can show, how I'd like to brighten your day?
If I could, and you must know I would, there is so much I would do.
But it's not up to me, I've made my choice, now it is up to you.

So much is out there in this world, waiting for a touch like yours.
From the highest alps to the whitest beaches, I can see you on those shores.
God put you here with a purpose in mind, and goals to make you care.
It's there deep inside of you, tucked away where only love will dare.
It is that drive from deep within, that won't let you give up the fight.
For I know, you know, in your heart of hearts, what to do that is right.
So here we are, it is another day back at your middle school.
And I admit things are a little different from when I learned the Golden Rule.

But some things never change, especially matters of the heart.
We still want to be accepted, to be liked, to be allowed to play a part.
To dream some dreams that are just for dreaming, once in a while.
To laugh a lot, to frown lots less, and to know what makes us smile.
We want to learn, to do really well, no matter what the test.

To be a special individual indeed, yet, fit in with all the rest.
We want to grow up, but not grow old, no matter what our age.
And we know a bird never really sings, as long as it is locked in a cage.

So if I could, and you know I would; I'd unlock your door.
I'd wish you peace and give you rest, and bring an end to your war.
I'd show you life on top of the clouds, up where the angels fly.
I'd give you wings to dream your dreams, so you'd never have to cry.
I'd sit back and watch as you climb higher and higher and begin to soar.
Knowing the freedom you now feel, watching you want it even more.
I know you can have it all, it is right with in your view.
I see you glide with a much clearer focus, yes, I believe in you.

There is potential you don't even realize, just beneath your skin.
The only real question I have is "When are you going to begin?"
You are so smart, and see life so deeply, mostly through your heart.
And that's okay, in fact, it is the very best place to start.
So set your goals high and dream your dreams true.
Don't let others knock you down, because people are counting on you.
And if you should fall short, or stumble along the way.
I'll be coming back real soon, to have our special day.
Where you can lean on me, and I can learn from you.
Because when the two of us are together, neither one of us is blue.

AWARDS AND OTHER STUFF
by John Achor

I have a thousand memories and mementos from the military which mean a great deal to me. I won't include my wife and children; they are at the top of the list—a given.

I earned a dozen Air Medals, most of them for a set number of missions hanging around the coastlines of countries like Vietnam and Russia. Included in the group are also a few flights flown against the French nuclear tests in the South Pacific. One Air Medal was awarded for a single flight where we captured the signal of the HH, a suspected, yet previously unknown Cold War radar. According to the award's criteria, this action qualified for the Distinguished Flying Cross. However, politics being what they are—yes, even in the United States Air Force—the grand gurus of awards converted this one into an Air Medal. Though all the Air Medals appear the same, I'm proud to have piloted the plane when those guys in the back captured that new radar signal.

In the summer of 1969, I took one of the Alaskan RC-135Ds to Kadena Air Base, Okinawa—now part of Japan. My crew and plane were to fill a gap in the RC-135M fleet stationed there because those aircraft were long overdue for major overhauls. The M's had fan jet engines; we didn't. They could refuel in level flight after takeoff; we couldn't. These conditions caused headaches and heartburn for the staff, but as usual the crews get the job done--despite the staff. The missions were nineteen and a half hours long and we flew, without crew augmentation, every three days for the best part of a month. We completed our assignment, but this accomplishment was not the one affording me the fondest memory.

Back in those days, one of the popular half-hour TV sitcoms was "F-Troop." The show starred Forrest Tucker as a U. S. Calvary Sergeant in the old west. Our Kadena maintenance crew nicknamed themselves after the television show. I own a small, handmade certificate making me an honorary member of F-Troop—in my mind, it's a real tribute.

Leaving my Alaskan assignment, the Security Service Maintenance Commander presented me with a small award—a 5" x 7" framed photo of one of our planes. It was overlaid with a Security Service patch, a thank you and it was signed by the "Chief Wire Bender." Another memento that rates a spot on my wall of honor.

I received a similar award when I left the Joint Reconnaissance Center in the Pentagon. The standard presentation was a fancy 9 x 12-inch photograph of the Pentagon with space around the sides for others in the JRC to add comments and signatures. I appreciated the effort, but there was another that means more to me. Another 5" x 7" award, hand drawn and typed. It was signed by all the officers and NCO members of the Watch Team I worked with. There's a spot on my wall for this one as well.

Do self awards count? In this instance, I think this one does. In the olden days, the steering wheels of cars were held in place with a single nut, and to cover it, builders installed a steering wheel cap. Be patient, all will reveal itself in due course. During my tour in Alaska, we spent about a week each month at Shemya Air Base in the Aleutian chain of islands, flying a one-of-a-kind airplane. The crew chief and maintenance staff believed she was the Cadillac of the fleet. They added a Cadillac steering wheel cap to each of the pilots' yokes. Landing at thirty minutes into the day of January 13, 1969, I found, later, the runway was too slick for us to stop. We went over a forty-foot cliff, but all 18 on board walked away.

The crew chief entered the wreckage and salvaged those Cadillac wheel caps and gave them to me. I asked if they could procure a piece of the aircraft skin. They presented me with a chunk of aluminum about two feet by three feet, almost too big to stash in my A-3 bag—a rather voluminous zippered canvas container for flight gear.

In my basement back at Eielson Air Force Base, I cut 18 three-inch rectangles from the aluminum skin. I fashioned and stained 18 oak plaques. To every plaque, I attached an engraved plate containing one person's name and the date "13 Jan 1969" as well as a piece of the airplane skin. Two of the plaques were larger than the rest so they could also accommodate one of those Cadillac wheel caps. One of these went to my copilot and I kept the other. Another reserved spot on my wall.

Speaking of my copilot on that flight, after losing track of one another's whereabouts, we located each other on the internet a couple of years ago. I always knew this Air Force Academy graduate was a talented officer and if he stayed on active duty long enough, he would outrank me—he did. I always did my best to pass on knowledge and skill to those who worked for me, but never thought of it past that. In his email note to me, he included me in a group who affected his life and career—and considered me a mentor. Awards are not always tangible objects with a spot on the wall.

This final one needs a bit of background also. Before I moved to my Alaskan assignment, I attended an advanced Survival School at Fairchild Air Force Base at Spokane, Washington. This was a special course designed for strategic reconnaissance aircrews with much of the material classified above Top Secret. Even the names of the clearance levels were classified. To be a member of the school staff required clearances to these levels and extensive background checks. One of the senior Non-Commissioned Officers was a Master Sergeant — which as I recall, was the highest NCO rank available at the time. He began his military career during World War II in the German Wehrmacht. When his unit was overrun on the eastern front, he was conscripted into the Russian Army. The war over, he crawled under triple concertina barbed wire and made his way to U. S. occupied territory.

Proceeding to the United States, he joined our Air Force and rose to the rank of Master Sergeant. His distinctive voice, a growling guttural sound and his trademark gesture were ominous. From a fist, he extended his first and second fingers pointing forward and curved downward like a serpent's fangs. There was a sound to accompany the hand gesture and we called him the Snake—not to his face as I recall.

Our accommodations were sumptuous. An abandoned underground ammunition bunker was *home,* and was modified with "rooms" made of plywood. The cubicles extended the length of the bunker on both sides and a door which could be locked from the outside. Each compartment was tall enough to stand erect, but only thirty inches square. Resting was accomplished by leaning into a corner. We were not allowed to communicate with other "captives."

To be sure we remained silent, guards slipped into the pitch-black quarters and listened. Offenders were removed from their cells and subjected to extra interrogations. On occasion, the Snake would enter and make his presence known.

Even recognizing his voice, and knowing he was really on our side, a chill went up my spine at the sound of his voice.

Part of our training took place in a group compound. The course was too short to prepare a full-blown escape, but we were to make a concerted effort to plan one. On occasion, the guards would put canvass bags over our heads and march a line of hooded prisoners—who knows where. On other occasions, we were selected for interrogations. Placed in a small room with a table, two chairs and the inquisitor, we were to avoid giving up any substantive information to these interrogators.

At the end of the course, each student was debriefed by one of the staff. I drew the Snake. Rather than sitting behind the desk, he slid his chair to the side. The position allowed him to use the corner of the desk and sit closer to me. He covered all the items on the out-processing checklist and then we chatted for a few minutes. At last, he held out his hand to me. As we shook, he said, "I would work for you."

We stood and I left the room. I hope I at least muttered a "thank you," but I'm not sure. From a man with such a background, I consider his words as high praise indeed. It was not a tangible item for my wall, but I think it is the greatest award I ever received.

MY RELIGION OF THESE DAYS

by John Petelle

I exit my door,
offer myself to the night.
My leather shoes float above the sidewalk,
organic whispers, showcasing
the perfect cadence of my steps.

Nineteen blocks of pilgrimage, and I am here:
El Templo Celebrar.
The ten pm breeze strokes the silk of my shirt,
rippling,
a red flag announcing my arrival.

My clothing is a noise that does not recognize rules,
or curfew.
It refuses the ordinary.
Exotic and exemplary,
It is as I am.

Thirty yards of normals wait their turn.
At the entrance,
Esteban holds the rope,
waves me inside with his ivory smile.
His shift ends at midnight.

By two,
he will become salsa on the main stage.
We may dazzle the crowd together.
They have marvelled at our duet before,
bowed before our beauty.

Carlita appears at my side,
two glasses held,
swaying,
amused invitation
in her bright emerald eyes.

I have seen her hypnotize a dance floor,
her long skirt,
a river that drowns all watchers
as her currents display golden beaches,
promise treasures of the delta.

We tip our drinks back, embrace,
and I glide onwards,
inhaling wild perfumes,
the desire
from untamed humanity under colored lights.

The outsiders
cannot hide how obvious they are,
whether leaning on the bar,
or flinging themselves to the club's center,
desperate worshippers of an unfamiliar mythology.

No matter.
They are welcomed here by we:
the magnificent gods of dance,
the brazen goddesses of release.
We will baptize the strange ones
with vodka kisses and whiskey touches.

Perhaps I will celebrate one of them,
enter my home with a stranger
at four am,
watch the dawn
cast them from my bed.

Perhaps I will not.
It does not matter.
The urgency is the music,
the movements here, in my temple,
where I am reborn each day.

FROM OMAHA TO DA NANG – MY SEARCH FOR A SPIRITUAL HOME IN VIETNAM

by John Costello

St. Mary medal and JMJ prayer were my shield against danger and stress in Vietnam. *"John Costello I never go into chapel without praying for you. Pray for me. Union in Christ."* –Sr. Elisabeth Sacred Heart Orphanage, Da Nang.

Out of 2.7 million Americans who served in Vietnam, I imagine there are very few who hopped on a sampan boat searching for a Trappist Monastery in China. And became forever friends with Sister Elisabeth, a Vietnamese nun at Sacred Heart Orphanage Da Nang. My hero Father Capodanno Lt. USN visited here in April 1966 same month and year as my visit. Fr. Capodanno was killed rescuing Marines in combat and a Medal of Honor recipient. Given my loving Catholic upbringing, friendship with Sr. Elisabeth and Sr. Magdalena, my "Angels of peace" were the relief I needed from war, trauma and homesickness.

October 1, 1965, I flew on a C-130 with 90 Sailors and Marines from Clarke USAF Base in the Philippines to USAF Base in Da Nang, Vietnam. This was the first day of my 12-month tour of duty in Da Nang. President Johnson and Defense Secretary McNamara had this plan in 1965 to escalate the war against the Viet Cong and North Vietnamese Army and win the war in six months as reported by the media. I was one of few Navy sailors sent for in-country, shore duty.

My dad, James, saw it coming. In summer of 1964, Dad and I visited a Navy recruiter in Omaha. The Navy recruiter looked tall and handsome in his dress white uniform. Dad looked like Ralph Kramden in his work uniform and blood stained boots as butcher at Offutt USAF Base. The recruiter said he would send me to Radio School in San Diego. Dad saw it coming. "You are going to send my son to Vietnam not to any Radio School." I winced when he said that. In November 1964, I finished my Navy Bootcamp in San Diego. Next, I got great shore duty and on the job training in radio operations at Naval Air Station Pt. Mugu, California. My friend Ben (retired Lt. Col USA) said, "This ocean beach side base is like a resort. How did you get this?"

Then just as Dad said, I got orders for Vietnam. As my departure day approached, Dad said, "God is the 'Higher authority' in life and war in Vietnam, not President Johnson." My mom, Lucille, prayed JMJ prayers every night with our family of ten and Dad taught us about Fr. Thomas Merton and Bishop Sheen from the 40 books he read written by them. Also my 13 years of Catholic school and seminary with Dominican/Benedictine priests and nuns taught us to put "JMJ" and "A.M.D.G." on our homework and exams. This strong Catholicism shielded me from stress in Vietnam and like a magnet directed me to search for the Catholic Church, orphanage and nuns in Da Nang and Trappist Monastery in Hong Kong, China.

Right away upon arrival at USAF base Da Nang we were herded like cattle onto military buses with handrails, no seats and metal screen instead of windows. We drove several miles through streets of downtown Da Nang with an awful smell from fresh fish and food markets and odor from the harbor port. With shock I saw rats as big as a small dog. There were people yelling at us in Vietnamese. My imagination ran wild. "Are we going to get killed riding on this bus? I wondered. My adrenalin was on high alert. I grabbed my dog tags and St. Mary medal and prayed silently a little JMJ prayer my dad taught me. "Jesus, Mary and Joseph we love you save souls." As the bus moved slowly and sometimes stopped in congested traffic, I heard young children yelling in Vietnamese and English; "Marines No. 1, Navy number 10 thou... Navy dinky dou (English –crazy). Navy boo coo dinky dou!" What is this I said to myself... these boys are messing with us. Their taunts made me laugh, broke my tension, calmed me and reduced my fear. A few guys on bus cheered, laughed, and waved at the kids.

Finally, our bus reached its destination and our 40 sailors reported to U.S. Navy APL-30 (Nick-named the 'Dirty-30') a floating barracks/ship tied to deep water piers in Da Nang harbor in the South China Sea. Serving with NSA Da Nang, I was assigned to a Hatch Team (with hundreds of others) to work as a longshoreman/crane operator with every cargo from "beans to bombs" at deep water piers and on vessels in the South China sea. It was dangerous, dirty work.

We used to say, "Cargo handler requires a strong back, a weak mind and lots of muscles." Listening to Armed Forces Radio and songs from Johnny Rivers' "Memphis;" Petula Clark's, "Downtown;" Chad & Jeremy's "A Summer Song;" The Byrds' "Turn, Turn, Turn;" The Animals' "We Gotta Get Out Of This Place;" Barry McGuire's, "Eve Of Destruction;" Bobby Fuller's "I Fought The Law." Country music got us through monotonous, backbreaking work like rolling 500 pound bombs, hooking up Na Palm bombs, pallets of cement, tanks, etc.

Sometimes I walked down Da Nang streets with Army or Marines and they would say; "Look at that 'Gook over there…he is squatting and taking a dump just like a damn dog." It made me wince to hear this. Then I would see a 90 pound Vietnamese pedicab driver taking a 180-pound drunken sailor or marine to a skivvy-house or bar. I thought to myself, "No wonder some call us Ugly Americans."

During my first week and going to markets and talking to Vietnamese people, I found to my delight, Sacred Heart Cathedral Church, Orphanage and School in Da Nang. There were many hundreds of children adopted from this orphanage. One of the amazing things about this orphanage is that one of the sisters from the Convent before handing the Birth Registers to the new Government in 1975 –as requested to, managed to painstakingly copy by hand, all the names, birthdates and departure dates of 1600 children. Exploring the streets of Da Nang was not enough. The nuns at the orphanage and Sunday mass in Latin gave me complete emotional and spiritual relief from the chaos, trauma, homesickness and war. My girlfriend Pat's daily letters for 18 months, letters from family, friends and sixty fifth grade students from St. Philip Neri, Sr. Ruth Kelly and St. Pius Catholic Schools in Omaha also gave me great comfort and support. Every week we had 'mail call." Some guys called it "female call." We had no contact by phone with family and friends 10 thousand miles away in USA. So getting a letter, card or "care package' from home was like having your birthday, Christmas day, 4th of July all in one day. After mail call, we had to go right back to work. I would take my letter, shove it into my pocket and carry it like precious gold. I took it to my rack on APL-30. Before going to sleep I would read these cards and letters over and over and cherish every word. Then I put the letter under my pillow and fall asleep.

In October 1965, I still remember my first visit with Sister Magdalena, Director of Sacred Heart Orphanage-School Da Nang. The nuns were Sisters of St. Paul de Chartres who supervised the orphans and school. Sister was 5' tall and about 90 pounds in her white habit. She had a holy, charming smile, calm and warm greeting and presence that at once made me feel joyful, welcomed, and at home. She was highly educated, studied in France and was fluent in English, French, Tagalog, and Vietnamese. We became instant, best friends. I shook Sister's hand and she said, "Thanks God you Americans are here. At least you American Marines and Army will stand and fight the Viet Cong and enemy."

I asked Sister, "What do you mean… I do not understand what you ae saying."

Sister replied, "We don't trust the Vietnamese ARVN and National Guard. When the enemy comes, they (ARVN) run away and hide. At least you Americans will stay and fight."

I thought to myself: Well isn't that nice… we Americans traveled ten thousand miles from USA to fight for people in Vietnam and they do not trust or have faith in their own military. Sister's comment made me stop, reflect and question for the first time why are we Americans here fighting this war if native Vietnamese do not trust their own military? i.e. Why are we here? Should we be here?

Sister Magdalena introduced me to Sr. Elisabeth, one of her teachers. Sr. Elisabeth wearing her white habit, also 5' tall, had a beautiful face and her smile just melted me. Sr. Elisabeth was filled with holiness, love, peace, warmth, and joy. Each time I saw her, I felt I was in the presence of a saint. Her friendship, prayers, and support were my rock and anchor and helped me get through hard, lonely days during my year-long tour of duty in Vietnam. The nuns asked me to teach English to their grammar school students because I do not have an accent. Nebraska-- my home town was the home of Johnny Carson, Tom Brokaw and other TV stars who have no accents, unlike deep south Alabama, Texas or New York. I felt peace and joy with every one of my over 20 visits.

On many visits when I entered the orphanage grounds, I carried two bags of candy from local markets. Instantly over 20 orphan children surrounded me, jumping and cheering for candy. I brought my shipmate Carl and introduced him to the nuns and children. On one visit Carl asked, "Sr. Magdalena… what do you need?"

"I need a truck and lots of toothbrushes," she replied.

"I can't get you a truck Sister, but I'll get some toothbrushes" he said. For three weeks in December 1965, Carl and I went around on APL-30 and in Da Nang and we asked many Navy, Marines and Army guys to give a small donation in cash or MPC for Sr. Magdalena and the orphans at Sacred Heart. Carl wrote a letter to his mom in Ohio and requested toothbrushes for orphans in Dà Nang. His mother went to her corner Walgreens and bought every toothbrush in the store and sent them to Carl at NSA Da Nang, APL-30

A few days before Christmas 1965, Carl and I in holiday spirit made a visit to Sr. Magdalena at the orphanage. Carl handed Sister a large package of toothbrushes and an envelope with $550 in cash. Sister reacted at once… she choked up… could not talk… then tears filled her her eyes and rolled down her face. Carl and I hugged Sister. "For the children I thank you… more than words can say," she said. We exchanged Merry Christmas greetings. Sister said a short prayer," God bless you and good bye." Carl and I left the orphanage in a happy Christmas holiday spirit.

There are many people who come and go in our lives. A few touch us in ways that change us forever, making us better from knowing them. Sr. Elisabeth, a nun and teacher, at Sacred Heart School in Da Nang made a huge difference in my life… and for this I am grateful. I still carry a photo of Sr. Elisabeth and I consider her a life-long cherished, spiritual friend. More than anyone in Vietnam, she kept me emotionally and spiritually grounded with her daily prayers, warm greetings, cherished smile and caring, happy demeanor. We shared happy visits, talks and prayers together. Also, she had me talk and read English to her class at Sacred Heart School.

"John Costello, I never go into Chapel without praying for you. Union in Christ "Sr. Elisabeth. "John Costello, Pray for me. Inion in Christo." Sr. Elisabeth. "John Costello, Virgin Mary protect and bless your ideal life of Seminarist. Sincerely, Sister Elisabeth." Sr. Elisabeth wrote these words to me on postcards, holy cards and bookmarks which I keep to this day. She was a harmonious, deeply religious nun who was caring, kind, warm, full of joy, and spiritual wisdom. I pray for Sr. Elisabeth and Sr. Magdalena that our Lord Jesus, Lady of Fatima bless and protect them and will help me find and reunite with them. Sr. Elisabeth and Sr. Magdalena my "Angels of peace" were the relief I needed from war, trauma, and homesickness.

R & R visit in 1966 from Da Nang to Trappist Monastery Near Hong Kong

After joining the military, many soon learn to avoid volunteering because you can end up doing cleanup, picking up cigarette butts or some working-party detail lifting, carrying boxes. In June I was with a group of five shipmates when a Navy Lt. came by and yelled: "I need some volunteers… to go on a 20-day 'R & R" on a Navy attack-cargo ship to Hong Kong, with stops in Philippines, Okinawa and Taiwan." This will get me out of Vietnam for 20 days…I just won the lottery… I don't care where this ship goes… I'll get out of her for 20 days … I said to myself. God blessed me once again with another miracle. "Thank you Lord Jesus," I prayed for allowing me to be in the right place at the right time. All Americans

serving in Vietnam were offered 5 days "Rest and Recreation" also known as "R
& R." We had about ten places to choose from including: Tokyo, Hong Kong,
Bangkok, Australia, Manila, Singapore. I chose Hong Kong. Some guys chose to
stay in Vietnam or travel to Hawaii. That made no sense to me. Bob Joes, our
navy postal clerk in Da Nang, listed five places in Hong Kong he planned to
visit. "How did you learn about these pagodas, museums and Kowloon in Hong
Kong," I asked.

"I read several magazines on Hong Kong" he replied. From talking with Bob
and reading his magazines I found a Trappist Monastery in Hong Kong.

In June of 1966, I traveled for 20 days 'R & R' from Da Nang to Hong Kong
with 80 Marines, Army, Air Force and Navy on the USS Tulare, a Navy attack
cargo ship. The trip was over 1100 miles through the South China sea. "We
are going to do some bar hopping, get wasted, and find some cute Asian girls,"
said some shipmates. " I'm searching for a Trappist Monastery and some monks.
Would anyone like to join me?" I replied. I got no answer.

By talking to hotel people and some taxi drivers in Hong Kong, I learned I
could take a sampan boat from Hong Kong to Trappist Monastery Lantau Island.
"Sampan ride to Lantau will take you about 30 minutes," said a Taxi driver.

In the harbor pier, I found a sampan boat with a Chinese man and woman
who looked to be in their forties. "We can take you to Lantau for 20 bucks,"
they said. I agreed and hopped in their boat. From the sun they had dark-tanned
skinned and wrinkled faces. They each weighed about 90 pounds soaking wet in
their black pajamas. The sampan was a relatively flat bottomed boat, with a small
shelter and roof on board. It had oars and a small motor. I think it was their home
on inland waters. There was a small 12" red wooden Buddha statue with a dish
holding a cigarette and a pear. There were pots, pans, and a container with tea.
They both chain smoked cigarettes with a strong odor. They offered me tea and
cookies. The Chinese boat people spoke enough English to take me to Lantau
Island and told me how to get back to Hong Kong.

After my arrival at Lantau Island, I paid the boat people, thanked them for
the tea and got out of boat. I walked a short distance, less than a mile, on a scenic
trail to the monastery. The Trappist haven Monastery Our Lady Of Joy Abbey is
a monastery located on the hills of scenic and serene north eastern part of Lantau
Island, Hong Kong. I was in a euphoric state upon arrival at the monastery and
during my whole visit. I imagined my dad, James, next to me. It would be dream
of a lifetime for him.

I entered an office door in front of this huge monastery wall and met a priest/monk dressed in brown habit about 6'tall and skinny. "My name is John Costello from Nebraska, serving in the Navy, visiting from Da Nang, Vietnam on a 'R & R' vacation in Hong Kong," I said. "My dad James has read over 40 books by Fr. Thomas Merton, a Trappist Monk. I am a former Benedictine seminarian and had over 13 years of school with Dominicans and Benedictines," I said.

"My name is Father Joe (Joseph). I am from Wisconsin. We are Cistercian Trappist priests and brothers. All of our priests and brothers are cloistered and do not meet or talk to the public except me. As the PR priest, I coordinate the sale of our Trappist bottles of milk to the public to help fund our monastery and support our community of monks," he said as he warmly shook my hand and welcomed me into his office.

My dad taught me to love baseball and since the age of five, I had collected hundreds of baseball cards as a kid. My friend Hugh and I always quizzed each other on Mantle, Mays, etc. "Father Joe, since you are from Wisconsin, what do think of the Braves moving from Milwaukee to Atlanta:" I asked.

"Milwaukee!!! The Braves were in Boston… Boston Braves. I never heard they were in Wisconsin," he said. At that point we had a disconnect. I was ignorant on baseball history and did not know Milwaukee Braves started as Boston Braves. We were both silent for a few moments since our dialogue did not make any sense.

"When did you leave Wisconsin for Lantau Monastery"" I asked.

"It has been over 20 years since I left Wisconsin. I have not watched TV, listened to radio or read newspapers and magazines for decades." Fr. Joe then told me some history. "The Trappist Haven Monastery in Lantau Island, Hong Kong was established by Roman Catholic Monks of the Strict Observance, or Trappists, after fleeing from regime in Peking in 1956. It was built in European medieval style using stones. The monastery is the only one of its kind in Hong Kong. There is a Chapel with bright airy interior and landscaped gardens perfect for meditation and prayer." We toured the grounds and monastery building. We walked around a second level balcony of the chapel and looked down at over 20 monks with balding hair, wearing brown habits praying Divine Office and singing a Gregorian chant. It was a very peaceful and heartfelt, solemn moment for me to witness with Trappist monk Fr. Joe.

Out of 2.7 million Americans who served in Vietnam, I imagine there are few who had this experience. "The monks are from Asia, USA, and Europe" said Fr. Joe. We walked around landscaped gardens and Father took me back to his office where we had tea, crackers and cheese. (After all Fr. Joe was from Wisconsin, the cheese state.) Fr. Joe gave me two bottles of milk marked with a red Trappist logo. We said a prayer together. Father gave me his blessing; we hugged, and I left Lantau Island and went back to the noise, sights, smells and sounds of people, markets and pagodas of Hong. Kong.

I called Dad and Mom from my hotel in Hong Kong. The Red Cross helped with the long-distance call and it was 2 a.m., Omaha time when the call was made. My parents had not heard my voice in nine months and because the Red Cross introduced the call, my parents were shocked and scared that I was injured or killed in Vietnam. They were excited and happy when I said I just called to say hello, and I was sending a Trappist logo milk bottle to them from my recent visit to Trappist Monastery in China.

Shortly after Hong Kong, our R & R group returned to Vietnam. I was very depressed after enjoying the Trappist Monastery and the people, sights and sounds of China, Taiwan, Okinawa and Philippines. Daily prayer, my Saint Mary medal, Sunday Mass in Latin and Vietnamese, letters from home, weekly visits to Sacred Heart school with Sr. Elisabeth, the Trappist Monastery visit, gave me a respite and a shield from the chaos of war in Vietnam. In 2004 St. Mary Pius OP age 80, a Dominican principal from my St. Philip Neri grammar school in Omaha, took me to the grave of Father Thomas Merton (my dad's hero) in Kentucky. I think of my shipmate Ralph (who said to me many times the USA should not be in Vietnam) each time I hear the 1965 song: "Eve of Destruction" by Barry McGuire and "We gotta Get out of This Place" by the Animals. Ralph, Carl and I heard these songs on radio as we unloaded 500 pound bombs and other cargo in the South China Sea in Vietnam. Deo gratias.

Sister Elisabeth, Sr. Magdalena and Vietnamese Sr. Carolyn O.C.D. nun San Diego 2017 -2018.

Through a miracle and several visits in 2017-2018, my daughter Laura and I met Sr. Carolyn O.C.D. a cloistered nun at the Carmelite Monastery in San Diego. "I was born in South Vietnam in 1975. After the war my dad was taken to a Communist re-education prison. I did not see my dad until I was 12 years old. He was released from prison and came back to our home in 1987. I was scared of this man. I did not know who he was. I ran to my sisters. My older sister Carolyn took me and said, "We are safe; he is our dad."

During my Sunday visits with Sr. Carolyn and Sr. Yvonne (a Carmelite nun for 64 years), I told them about my military service in Vietnam. Then I told them about my cherished friendships with Sr. Elisabeth and Sr. Magdalena at Sacred Heart Orphanage Da Nang. I asked Sr. Carolyn, since she still has family in Vietnam, if she could help me find these two nuns. I would love to contact them. "I will try to find them John and let you know," Sister said.

In February 2018 after 4 pm Sunday Mass, Laura and I had our usual visit with Sr. Carolyn and Sr. Yvonne. At once Sr. Carolyn said, "John, I have some good news to tell you." Sr. Carolyn radiated with joy and love. "John, I contacted the Catholic Bishop of South Vietnam, and he found the convent of Sr. Elisabeth and Sr. Magdalena. I am sorry to tell you they have both passed away. There are still two or three nuns living in a retirement home who knew them at Sacred Heart. The good news John is Sr. Elisabeth and Sr. Magdalena are now praying for you in heaven," Sister said.

On February 20, 2018, through another miracle, I met Sr. Cecilia O.C.D. a cloistered Carmelite nun in Alhambra, California. We have sent and received over 100 emails, letters, and cards through the U.S. Post Office. She is my little sister in Christ, and spiritual counselor and fills a big hole in my heart since I cannot contact Sr. Elisabeth in Vietnam. Sr. Cecilia has been a Carmelite nun for 27 years is a skilled reader and writer and fluent in Spanish and English. Deo gratias.

DA NANG SUNSETS

by John F. Costello

Along with daily prayer to Jesus, Mary and Joseph, there were weekly visits with Sr. Elisabeth and Sr. Magdalena, nuns at Sacred Heart Church and Orphanage in Da Nang, Vietnam. This was the same orphanage visited by my hero, Father Vincent Capodanno, Lt., recipient of the USN Medal of Honor. When there were not monsoon rains, I observed the hand of God with the most amazing, spectacular, colorful sunsets in Da Nang. They were the most beautiful I have seen anywhere in the world, giving me great peace, comfort, and joy. At sunset I could see amazing colors of blue, violet, brown, tan, yellow bouncing off the ocean waters of Da Nang beaches and harbor ports and piers. After my year in Vietnam, I have visited 40 of the 50 states. I also visited Ireland, Germany, Canada, Mexico, the Philippines, Okinawa, Hong Kong, Taiwan and Honduras, but I have never seen sunsets as beautiful, colorful or breathtaking as Da Nang, Vietnam.

Montagnards, Pastor Scott from Ohio and Rites of Passage.

On some Saturday nights, we had an outdoor movie on land in front of the "Dirty 30" APL-30, a floating barracks. It was like being at a drive-in movie in USA but instead of being in a car, we sat on folding chairs near APL-30. Some local Vietnamese of all ages in downtown Da Nang watched the movie from across the street. I am not sure if they could hear or understand English but most stayed and watched anyway.

Most movies were cowboy westerns with stars like John Wayne. One time during an action movie, we had Viet Cong snipers shooting at us with bullets going through the movie screen. At first we all thought it was part of the movie. Then several officers and NCOs (non-commissioned officers) yelled, "Hit the deck; they (the enemy) are shooting at us." I was annoyed because the movie was at a critical part. I could feel the wind of bullets fly over my ear as I fell and hit the ground. We never did see the ending.

One Saturday night we had a visitor, Pastor Jeff Scott from Akron, Ohio. He showed us a video he shot while doing Christian missionary work with Montagnards in Vietnam. "Montagnards are dark skinned, primitive mountain tribes in the Central Highlands in Vietnam. "Some have become Protestant Christians," said Pastor Scott.

I was shocked and stunned when I talked to Vietnamese of all ages on the streets of Da Nang to see their smiles revealed jet-black teeth. I learned from older Vietnamese women that the black teeth were the result from the habit of chewing betel nut. A 67 year-old Hanoian woman dressed in a loose silk over blouse, black silk trousers said chewing betel nut is a common custom in Vietnam. Betel chewing releases a mild stimulant that relieves tooth aches and suppresses the appetite. "Besides blackening teeth some Vietnamese boys and girls from ages 12 to 14 would have their top two front teeth filled to the gum as a rite of passage," said Pastor Scott. "For Montagnards the rite of passage, i.e. going from childhood to adult, was having front teeth removed. This showed they are superior to cows and all animals because animals are not smart enough to remove their front teeth," said Scott.

The video clearly showed a 12 year-old dark skinned girl lying on the ground while two adults held her and filed her teeth to the gum, without anesthetic, with a metal file like you would find in a machine shop. "I have never seen such bravery as this little girl, who weighed about 70 pounds, endure such pain through this gruesome rite of passage ritual," said Scott. The 30 of us military watching this video in front of APL-30, winced and grimaced in our chairs as we watched this tortuous ordeal.

ON WRITING

by Sara Hollcroft

I am a writer. I write. "My name is Hilda Rechless; you are to call me Mrs. Rechless." I was in 4th grade. "Today you will write an essay about your summer." I was given that same assignment from her the previous year as she taught both 3rd and 4th graders in our small school. A year earlier, I had not proven myself as a writer. Now, I knew what to say and how to write it especially since this summer I had stayed with my grandparents in Wymore. After all, they lived three blocks from the city pool, and the city pool was livelier than my regular summer routine of pulling weeds from the strawberry patch. As quickly as the weeds died after I pulled them, so did the words I wrote in last year's essay. I wanted to show my teacher, my role model, that I had been working on my writing skills over the summer.

I am a writer. I write. In the early mornings when sleep eludes my mind and body, I sometimes think back on that 4th grade summer writing assignment. I couldn't wait to put in poetic prose the wonder of that summer. Mom had purchased a swimsuit covered in yellow circles and red flowers just for me. It was the first one I had ever owned, and Mom knew I would remember that first summer staying alone with Grandpa and Grandma. I wanted Mrs. Rechless to feel the awe and excitement that I had felt when the cooling water coursed its way between my toes as I swayed my feet back and forth, circling left to right, right to left, over and over, back and forth in the pool. I wanted her to read about my fascination on how the water beaded on my feet and ankles and sparkled in the sunlight. She needed to know how much nicer it was in that pretty blue water and not the muddy water of our creek behind our house. I wanted her to know what the water looked like when the little boy to my left peed in the pool and the strong yellow of his pee quickly swirled around him ever so gracefully and then disappeared around the other boys innocently playing tag with him.

I am a writer. I wrote. On that early September Thursday of my 4th grade year, I poured out my love for my grandparents for letting me stay with them, my mom for buying me the most beautiful swimsuit that was ever made, and my absolutely wonderful summer, cooling off in the prettiest water God had given His children. I was so happy that Mrs. Rechless asked me about my summer and that I got to share my story with her. I knew that she would be proud of me since I was her best student in English the year before. Hadn't I won every diagraming sentences contest she gave? Hadn't I been her best speller? This year I would be the best writer she had ever had since I had actually had a fantastic summer to write about.

I am a writer. I wrote. I went beyond the 100 words she asked her class to write because I was on a mission to let her know every last detail. Details are important, you know. I remembered Mrs. Rechless telling us last year but I did not have the details to make my writing stand out, and unfortunately, had not developed an imagination to improvise.

But I had worked on details that summer. I took notice by using all of my senses whenever I entered a room or was outside. I mentally practiced writing phrases to describe my thoughts over the summer. So, now faced with the same assignment as last year, I wrote and wrote and wrote. I was the last one to hand in my essay. I wanted it to be on top, so she would read it first. As she clipped the essays together, she thanked us for sharing our summers with her and said she was looking forward to reading them that night. I nodded; she nodded back at me.

I am a writer. I write. I didn't sleep that night, knowing that my teacher was smiling as she read our papers. I couldn't wait until Mom called me to breakfast, but then I couldn't eat. I willed the big yellow school bus to come early for my brother and sisters and me. I could already see that large red A on my summer essay, but I also needed it in my hands and for my teacher to publicly praise my writing. I purposely wore my pink striped dress that day since its flared skirt would look nicely as I curtsied in thanks for Mrs. Rechless declaring I had written the best paper.

I am a writer. I wrote. I got my paper back.

I am a writer. I wrote and I write. Today, while reading my words, and in the words of Russian author and critical reviewer Vladimir Nabokov, would Hilda Rechless notice and fondle the details of my summer*[sic]*? Would she read my essay with "impersonal imagination and artistic delight"? (Nabokov) Would she have chills up her spine to tingle her imagination? Did I light the fires of delight, wonder, and remembrance through my story, my lesson?

Today I write, and as I put pen to paper or fingers to the keyboard, my writing muse shows me Mrs. Hilda Rechless standing in front of me in her Thursday's blue A- line dress with its second button from the top hanging precariously by a thread or two. As I looked forward to words of encouragement about my writing, I am still confused how that button can still be functional all these years. The words that I have been waiting years to read will have to wait again. I still see her small, red cursive words on top of my paper: *"You need to indent your paragraphs."*

APRIL 2, 2017: OUR TRUTH TODAY

Jen Stastny

In movies, heart monitors beep, beep, beep.
On the ninth floor of this hospital tower, they are
silent but no less insistent.

Peeking from behind an IV stand
the squat box of luminous lime numbers
informs me it is not time to worry.

My mother eats roast beef with gravy
in her hospital bed
and fusses with wires relaying observations
from her flesh to the box to unseen humans
whose jobs are numbers.

On another floor, they focus on
normal versus abnormal
while we, on this floor, think next steps to remain in the present,
to not project fictions of tomorrow's maybes on our hearts.

At midnight, her heart rate was 26.
Now, transitioning day nurse to night nurse,
"At 6:30 a.m. she experienced a 5.82 second ventricular standstill."
That means no pulse.

But the fierce, fighting heart of my little mom
restarted and righted herself, as my mom always has.

And now:
Resting - 66 b.p.m.
Eating - 81 b.p.m.
Sneezing - 94 b.p.m.

These are my hours to fluff and move pillows,
to adjust wires,
to text whomever she tells me to text and what,
to occasionally peer at the numbers, and
to remember this is life.

UNDER THE DESK

by Mandy Kottas

You can't hear her; she made sure of that.
It's not like you speak anyway.
She's new at this: hiding so much pain,
But she learned how to keep her place.

She can't see you; her body made sure of that.
You're too much to process.
"Maybe someday," she hopes in vain,
She can't stay in this place.

It's that body that got her here; hiding under her desk.
That body now forever changed.
It's because of you, each of you.
Always in her face.

It brings her down, under the desk.
Hiding from her shame.
Knowing you will never know.
She can't say his name.

It's her body that got her here, standing out from the rest.
She wanted beauty, but so did you.
Another hole to slide into.
Somewhere to hide from the rest.

And in that hole, she thinks of you.
Hiding under the desk.

You can't see it; the panic inside
Every you-niform she sees.
She eats it all until she bursts.
But all you get is her best.

She has to remember, while you move on.
Hiding under the desk.
Mucus and panic manifest.
Hiding under the desk.

MORNING IN THE SANDHILLS

by Andy Gueck

Feet hit the floor, lights out to avoid waking the house,
Fumble into clothes, reach the kitchen,
Make coffee and start it to perk.
Stomp into boots.

Head outdoors to catch, groom, feed the horses and start the day.
Heave the saddles on, lead horses to the hitch rail.
It's 4:30 am.

Walk back to the house,
the stars still a glitter-covered blanket surrounding our world
the moon, long set, enhances the darkness.
A quick breakfast, eggs, bacon and toast; coffee,
strong, black, scalding,
Enjoy as the day will be long.

Dishes in the sink,
one last swallow of coffee,
"saddle up and move out."

A pasture, four miles square,
we split, on opposite sides of a ridge,
headed to distant corners.

Past cattle, slowly awakening,
arising and starting to graze.
In the cool of the morning,
a gentle wisp of steam rises from the animals.
Dew glistens on the prairie grasses and plants,
 cactus spires gleam like gems.

Rays of the sun slowly creep over the hills
leaving huge shadows across the landscape.
The birds, the sounds of cattle lowing,
the occasional hawk,
 the sounds of early morning.

I hear Dad and see his actions from his words,
carried in the stillness.
Reaching the apex of my corner,
I direct the cattle toward water.
Down the hills, the flat and the windmill beckon.

Cattle move, nose to tail,
Following traditions old as time.
Ruts, older than the bison herds,
still used,
always leading from graze
 to water and back.

As the cattle begin to move
toward new grass,
we ride in new directions
to clear other areas and when done
will have combed the pasture of all cattle.
 Our small bunches begin to combine
 and become a small cattle drive.
Out of the hills,
and on to the flats,
watching the livestock,

keeping them moving
toward our destination.

The sun, now higher in the sky,
Warming, heating the earth,
horses beginning to show sweat patches.
Jackets needed in the morning chill,
now removed
 tied behind saddles.
Drink of water, grateful for the canteen.

The herd of cattle,
a dust cloud following.
The slow plodding of a horse trailing the herd,
keeping them moving,
moving in a desired direction.

In the distance, light colored earth,
signaling a prairie dog town.
Concerning, but not dangerous.

A foreign noise,
ah ha, a livestock semi,
pulling through the gate.
Then another and in rapid succession, a
 total of six, long, silver boxes
pulled by bright red engines.
Lining up like cattle at a feed bunk,
waiting the arrival of the meal.
One backed to a loading chute.

The herd noticed, but unaffected,
continues forward.
As herders, we just follow and prevent escapes.
As the cattle approach the pens,
there is a hesitation,

but only minor
as they move into the confinement of a small corral.
The dew that was lovely in the early morning
was now gone.
Heat, sunshine, dust,
mirages shimmer in the distance.
The hills seem empty of life,
but I can hear the chirps of the dogs,
occasional cries of a prairie owl.
The cattle low, but continue to move.

As they fill the pen,
we move to close the gate
to begin the next stage.

We begin to load the trucks,
the drivers help.
Forty head to a load,
not fat,
but ready to leave grass.

Suddenly the world is again quiet,
no cattle, no trucks,
only the sounds of nature.
Again the birds can be heard,
the slow plod of horse hooves
slowly walking behind the horseman.
Gates left either open or closed, always as found.
Then the mounting and returning toward the house.
The day of cowboy time almost done.

It's 2:30 in the afternoon.
Still time to haul hay.

THE RIVER

by Sharon Robino-West

Thursday: The adrenalin rush hasn't stopped since the night we came back from our sunny trip to the islands just hours ago. Everyone warned us to get back home because it was coming.

"Quickly! Dump that suitcase full of vacation and make space for baby books, pictures, receipts, military and medical records. So many keepsakes that can't be replaced." Not enough room. Not enough time.

Friday morning: I dress quickly in darkness, thinking I'll head to work at the crack of dawn, only to race back mid-morning when the call comes out for sand-bagging. Rushing home down one-lane back roads, I dread what's to come.

And there she is, the river already lapping and lashing against the bottom of the railroad bridge to my right with no space between metal and water. My heart leaps into my throat as I lay the pedal of my car to the floor, crossing over the bridge, and hoping it holds. This can't wait. Save our town now.

Coasting into town, there are more cars than usual, more people. The volunteer firehouse doors are thrown open, airboats lined up for rescue. Don't think. Hesitation kills. Just start sand bagging. Years of buried military training kick into gear as I rush to meet everyone. Here's a shovel, a sandbag. Start filling, or start carrying. My mind says "do it now."

She carried on for three nights, that river. By Friday the water was so high we put all the furniture up on blocks in the house, just in case. Perhaps we could save something. I try not to think about the surveyor's comment that our house is situated four feet below the crest of the river. Trees, and barns, and dead cows roll by. As I turn away from it all, I realize there used to be an island out in the middle of this river, covered in trees full of nesting eagles. It was there for as long as I can recall. I suddenly notice it is completely gone.

Saturday: They say it will crest tonight for sure. Someone set up a check point to keep the looters out, and they screen me back into town, where I make it to the house. My husband is holed-up there, waiting. For two long days, he's refused to leave. Finally, the sheriff comes by, telling him, "I can't make you leave, but it's not safe." Meanwhile, I've been staying with friends nearby on higher ground. He remains with the rest of the guys in town, loyal to the brotherhood to the end.

I plead once more, "I can't stay here."

"And I can't leave," he says, as I walk away, camera in hand and tears in my eyes. Shooting the damage downstream works better for me than waiting. Waiting for what?

Taking the backroads out of town, I swing the car onto a vista near Buccaneer Bay where the highway is now impassable. Stopping near the top, my heart pumps in my ears. As I move in shock, I wonder - was that the last time I would see my husband, furious at him and shaking with tears? I am disgusted with myself for running away.

On Saturday night she indeed crested, five feet over flood stage. Quickly doing the math, I realize the Platte River came nine feet over what should have buried us. The waves churned and broiled, pushing sandbags halfway across the road, sticks and debris on one side, our front door twenty feet away on the other side of the temporary divide, dry and untouched.

Maybe we'll go for good the next time, or maybe we'll hold stubborn and stay. And maybe we won't have a choice.

DINNER AT CHEZ BASEMENT

by John Petelle

The metal doors of the freight elevator clanged open vertically, jaws with flaking grey teeth preparing to consume my date and me. Suzanne shuddered within the grasp of my right arm as the noise reverberated through my empty workplace.

"Craig, are you sure this thing is safe?" she asked. The 25 watt bulb flickered dimly from the bare electrical socket in the roof of the elevator. The irregular lightning alternately showed the splintered pine floor, and plunged the empty compartment into darkness. Suzanne leaned in closer to me, as if she could crawl inside my skin and leave me to face the shadows alone.

"Nothing to worry about," I said, flexing my arm around her to reinforce my presence. I led her within the confines of the elevator, and the control panel buzzed harshly as I pressed and held the button to send us down a floor. The oversized wooden box jerked into motion, and we were on our way to the basement.

I was taking Suzanne to the basement as a half-romantic, half-seductive plan. The deserted storage area didn't have much in the way of comfort, but it virtually guaranteed privacy. Few people had any reason to go down there, and with the stairwell blocked by the brickwork that had collapsed earlier in the week, the only way down was to use the freight car. All I had to do was lock the car down on this floor, and we would be guaranteed freedom from any surprise visitors.

I swung the picnic basket in my left hand as we exited into the basement itself. The weak light behind us cast wild designs onto a sprawl of disassembled desks and broken office chairs. Most of the flat surfaces were cluttered with a scattering of electronics, telephone handsets, and computer accessories that our IT department kept around just in case they might be useful.

Releasing Suzanne, I fumbled along the wall for the row of light switches. The one closest to me would turn on the main bank of fluorescent lights - not the romantic semi-darkness I had in mind at all. The center switch activated the pair of naked bulbs on either side of the elevator. I flicked that switch up, and twin pools of pale light extended out in front of us. I also flipped up the far switch, and carefully-substituted blue bulbs sprang to life over the work table and folding chairs that I had set up during my lunch a few hours ago.

A cheesy red-and-white checkered tablecloth covered the scratched surface of the table, and white china plates gleamed like circular ghosts in the sapphire-tinted light. Two bottles of merlot stood on either end of the table, unobtrusively whispering relaxation, and the prospect of pleasant company over the spaghetti dinner I carried in the basket. I figured two bottles set the right tone, inviting full glasses, without being intimidating. If needed, there was a trio of the same Beaujolais-Villages vintage tucked around the side of the battered filing cabinet positioned as an end table.

Suzanne giggled as she looked over the softly-lit tableau, "You went all out for this. Much cozier than reservations at one of the Italian restaurants in town." She tilted her head, and gave me a sly wink, "And none of this nonsense of luring me into your apartment on our first date, either.

I was glad the rush of color to my face wasn't visible to her. I gave a bow, and in a parody of a French accent said, "If mademoiselle would care to be seated at zee table, I weel open zee bottle of wine. Would mademoiselle care for breadsticks?"

She laughed, "Mademoiselle would indeed like breadsticks. Mademoiselle is starving!"

I placed the basket on the filing cabinet and began removing the contents: a ceramic dish holding steaming Bolognese sauce over angel hair pasta, a half-dozen slices of garlic bread wrapped in foil, four breadsticks covered with a red-and-white patterned dish towel that matched the tablecloth, a container of parmesan cheese, and two - practical if not elegant - water bottles. As I arranged the meal on the table between us, I casually glanced over at Suzanne to gauge her reaction.

Subtle or not, she caught my gaze, and smiled at me. "This is wonderful, Craig. I appreciate all of the effort you put into this. If you are half the dinner companion that you are a chef, I am going to have a very good evening."

The emphasis she placed on the word 'very', made me think that perhaps a trip to my apartment after dinner wasn't out of the question after all. I gave her a grin as I pushed the wrapped breadsticks towards her, and picked up the bottle opener to uncork the first bottle of wine.

"Oh, French wine even. Fancy!" she exclaimed as she picked up the unopened bottle, and turned it in her hands to examine the label. Are you a wine connoisseur as well?"

"Hardly," I laughed. "I can't get my head around all that nonsense of a drink having a 'mischievous nose' or 'hints of cherry varnished over layered overtones of oak'. All I care about is whether it tastes good without costing fifty bucks a bottle."

She chuckled as she pulled her chair out and sat down, "Oh, so now I'm not worth fifty dollars a bottle. That's a loss of brownie points for you, mister!" Her teeth gleamed as she looked up at me, and I couldn't help but think perhaps I'd actually gained points, rather than losing them.

Realizing I was still standing, I pulled my chair out, banging it into my knee in my rush to sit down. "Ouch! That looks like it hurt." Suzanne winked at me, "Do I need to kiss it and make it better?"

My eyes must have flown open as far as my mouth, and Suzanne roared with laughter, the sounds of her mirth echoing off the brick walls in the large area around us. "Keep your pants on, lover boy. This is still our first date—way too early for kissing." She winked again, leaned in my direction with a playful look, and stage-whispered, "Maybe later, we can discuss it."

I sent a thought to my throbbing knee, that was half-apology and half-gratitude. If slamming chairs into my tender flesh was what it took, then that was a price I was willing to pay.

I lifted the spaghetti dish lid, and served some of the aromatic sauce and pasta onto her plate first. Reaching back into the basket for the regular glasses, I filled them with water, and then poured wine into both of the crystal goblets next to our plates and silverware.

"You thought of everything," she murmured, as she lifted the burgundy liquid to her lips.

I lost my voice for a moment, transfixed by the vision of her lips parted around the edge of the glass, while the extended line of her neck flexed as she swallowed. "Thank you," I finally managed to force out of my mouth, lifting my glass to her in a toasting fashion. "To my lovely date this evening: if you had turned me down, I would be as blue as these lights."

My words caught her mid-swallow, and she choked with laughter, gasping for air as her other hand thrashed on the table. "Are you trying to kill me?" she asked, "Or just trying to get an excuse to use CPR on me?" Without waiting for a response, she drained off the last of her wine, and tilted the glass against the open bottle in silent request.

I stood to refill her glass, and then taking a long drink of mine, topped it off as well. I retook my seat, and we settled in to our dinner, making small talk about our activities at work that day, and some of the more sensational news headlines that had surfaced in recent hours.

The first bottle of wine was emptied before either of us had finished our first portion of spaghetti. I opened up the second bottle, and in a confidential tone said, "Not to worry. I've got a private wine cellar here, for when work requires me to day-drink. There's plenty more."

"Day-drinker? You should be ashamed of yourself, upstanding member of the tech startup community that you are. Still, if it ensures we have plenty of wine tonight, I'll give you a pass on that character flaw."

Reassured, I reached around the filing cabinet to bring out one of the reinforcements.

A low rumble vibrated through the floor, lasting for several seconds. "Gah, the construction crews never stop around here. Give it a rest, boys," I said. "They've been either tearing down or building up something for the entire five-plus years we've been located here. I'm so tired of the jackhammering, and the pounding, and..."

My complaint was cut off by another rumble, more pronounced this time and spanning nearly a dozen seconds. Suzanne reached out to steady the wine glass and the open bottle, her eyes a little too wide, and furrows appearing on her forehead. "It's past eight o'clock. Isn't that a little late for construction?" she asked.

"Maybe they are trying to hit deadlines, with the poor weather the last few weeks putting them behind schedule?" My voice rose a lot more than it should have, and I searched for some other reassurance to offer. "They've been tearing up some of the streets lately, really pounding away. Maybe they've gotten complaints about the daytime racket, and they are trying to get some of it done at night?"

"Too many apartments and dorms in this neighborhood. I'd think they would get just as many complaints at night," she said. Before I could respond, the floor underneath us shuddered again, shaking this time, not just vibrating. "Craig," Suzanne shrieked, "this isn't construction! This is an earthquake!"

I wanted to tell her that she was being silly—Nebraska doesn't have earthquakes, when the floor began to heave like the hull of a rowboat caught out during a storm. The empty wine bottle flew past my face, along with our glasses, dousing me with water and wine before shattering on the floor. A series of pops like muffled gunshots made a counterpoint to the low grinding, and all of the light bulbs burst in their sockets, swamping us in total darkness.

My yell drowned out Suzanne's, and I felt my chair sway and tip over, dumping me sideways to the floor. Something sliced at my face, and a slashing pain blazed across my cheek. Unconsciously, my hands reached out to get my balance, and a constellation of pain exploded in both palms, as broken glass gouged my skin.

The high-pitched screech of bricks scraping against each other was overwhelmed by a thunderous crack, that sounded like the building's foundation was shattering beneath us.

At last, there was a lull, and then silence broken only by a slow cascade of bricks falling, Suzanne's ragged breathing, and—I was ashamed to realize—whimpers of pain coming from my throat.

"Craig, are you hurt? Where are you?"

"Don't...don't come over here, Suzanne. There's broken glass everywhere."

"What happened to the lights? Where's the picnic basket? You put our phones in the basket, didn't you?"

"Owww, yes. Yes, the phones are in the basket. It's on the filing cabinet at the end of the table. But there's no reception down here."

"I'm not worried about reception right now. I just want my flashlight app." I heard tapping as Suzanne felt her way along the surface of the table. "Ewww, I just dragged my hand though the spaghetti sauce," she groaned. The tapping acquired a metallic tone as she located the filing cabinet. "It's not....there's nothing on the cabinet. Maybe the basket went over by you?"

I grimaced, and steeled myself to try and move without putting any more of myself into contact with shards of glass. A clamor arose, with the clattering sound of falling cement or bricks emanating from the darkness behind Suzanne. A pause, and then another tumbling mass falling....where? The echoes went on for seconds, and sounded like they were coming from a long ways down.

"Craig? What's that noise? What's falling? And why does it sound like it is falling so far? Are there any floors below this basement?"

"Not that I know of, but this is a really old section of town, and I suppose some of it could have been built on older buildings or foundations. Don't move until we get some light - I don't want you to stumble into a hole or something." I forced myself into a crouch, and slowly waved my hands in front of me, a few inches off the ground, hoping to blindly encounter the basket and our phones inside of it.

A clacking sound, and a scratching, like hard metal on cement, came from the same direction as the echoes of falling masonry. The clacking repeated, sounding somehow moist, like pebbles rubbing each other in shallow water, closer now than before.

"What's that noise? Have you found the phones? I really want some light now. I'm scared. I think we should get out of the basement right now. Can you get us over to the elevator?"

"I...I don't know, Suzanne," I felt a hysterical urge to wail, and I made my hands into fists, using the flare of pain to try and get control of myself. Suzanne's voice was shrill, and I had a feeling if either one of us started to lose it, we both would, and we wouldn't recover until the rescue workers came and dug us out. "I'm still looking for the basket. I haven't found the phone yet, but yeah, I think I could get us over to....."

My voice trailed off, as the damp rattling sounded again, even closer, almost where I imagined Suzanne to be sitting. Her scream surged out in the darkness, harsh and wordless. I heard thumping, and the crash of her chair being knocked over. The clacking noise ceased, and was replaced by the sound of something heavy being dragged over the floor, and all the while, Suzanne's scream continued, without a letup for breath, yet moving farther away.

"Suzanne! Suzanne! Stay where you are!" I cried, the soles of my dress shoes slipping in the pools of wetness on the floor. An instant of silence as Suzanne's scream turned into a ragged gasp for air, and in that interlude of quiet, I heard an awful, thick, ripping sound, and her voice resumed in a high squeal, even louder than before.

I scrambled towards her, and forgetting about the table in my panic, I floundered right into it, knocking it over, and landing awkwardly on top of it.

The dragging sound resumed, as Suzanne's frantic cries resolved back into a stream of words, "Help me, Craig! Help me! It...something grabbed me, and it bit me, and, and, help..." a muted thump—like a mallet striking a watermelon—cut her voice off, and now there was only the dull scrape of her body being pulled over the rough floor.

I moved forward, heedless of the memory of rocks falling into an open chasm, desperately trying to catch up to Suzanne. More clacking, farther ahead of me now, and a dreadful repetition of that meaty, rending sound. The shifting rattle of chunks falling down into the distance again, and then a low moan, now coming from some distance ahead—and worse—below me.

I fell to my knees, weeping, my mind a dizzy blank, heedless of the damage to my hands as I pounded them on the floor, driving bits of glass deeper. I don't know how long I sprawled there. Time seemed as absent as light. At last, I rose to my feet, and staggered off in the direction I thought the elevator was located.

A sunburst erupted in my eyes as I smacked headlong into a wall. I reeled, and stretched my hand out in front of me, glass tearing into my fingertips again as they collided with the wall. Through some perverse stroke of luck, I felt the call panel for the elevator with my mutilated fingers. Bending my hand backwards, I mashed the back of my wrist against the call button, and I heard it weakly buzz in response. Somehow, power of some sort remained to the elevator circuits.

I lurched to one side, grasping for the handles to open the freight doors that Suzanne and I had come through such a short time ago. My arm encountered the buckled metal of the doors sticking several feet out from the elevator shaft, and I fell to my knees again in despair. The structural trauma must have collapsed the elevator shaft somehow, forcing the car and the doors into the basement.

Out in the darkness, the clacking became audible again, moving inexorably in my direction.

I sat, paralyzed, and waited for it to find me. Waited to be reunited with Suzanne. Below.

TIME OF WAR

by Beverly Hoistad

"See this ribbon here over my breast pocket?" I see a pale, clean, huge hand, unwrinkled, fingernails too short, and just that one scar on the right thumb from the Exacto knife during a high school English project. My son fingers a stiff three-toned ribbon the size of a piece of gum pinned just above his left pocket. "This means we signed on during 'time of war'," he explains. I swallow, look hard at the ribbon thinking it's a pretty color combination, then blink a few times. He stands proudly in his new "Cracker Jack" uniform, compliments of Uncle Sam, the U.S. Navy, and his first paycheck. At 6'5", I can only hug, holding on to his middle, while carefully trying not to step on his size 14 polished boots. He feels very slender without the three layers of baggy clothing that was his uniform before. We're crowded in a hanger with 2,000 or so gabbing guests and 724 other new shouting sailors. Celebrating. Flashes from digital cameras and camcorders are all over the place. I remember to take some pictures. We've just watched an hour presentation celebrating eight of the hardest weeks he's ever faced.

Early, early that morning, before the sun breaks above the horizon, after an hour and a half of "processing," we are ready to go to the graduation area. We sit for over an hour on metal bleachers, talking, waiting, watching the crowd and many children. Two cell phones and a camera are lost under the silver bleachers and recovered with time, ingenuity and sweat. Several small children run around, head to the bathrooms, bump into backs, and tussle with family and surrounding guests. Handicapped parents and grandparents arrive from a different door and are seated in set-up chairs on the floor. One pregnant woman toddles to the restrooms. A few retired Navy men sit in places of honor at the front of the crowd.

As the Naval band assembles and the flag bearers carry each of the fifty state flags, people hurry to their seats. A twenty-minute video commences, showing just what the recruits have done: arrival at O'Hare, an hour bus ride to camp, a week of processing where the kid with the longest hairiest head getting shaved gets a big laugh, classes, physical training, firefighting, battle stations, a few interviews with generals and a little propaganda for the present administration. When the hanger door opens, it's way too slow as we all crane our necks and look through the gaping hole. I hear marching feet, cadence called, shouts and whistles from the excited crowd. It's been nearly nine weeks since we've seen our babies. People are wiping tears from their eyes, men and women, indiscriminately. My daughter, my husband, me, too, as the first division marches by. The second and then the third division enter. We all search for the tallest one, the one we've traveled so far to see. Being a section leader, he's the third one in the third division he's told us in advance. He is. We follow him with our eyes until he marches out of sight down the huge room, and then comes back to stand in front of us. Each of the nine divisions marches in proudly, a Navy sea. Section leaders collect raincoats as there was a major downpour on the walk over from their ship: a christening? Next is a parade of flags, a rifle demonstration, awards, pomp and circumstance. Then, all of a sudden, it's over. Anchors aweigh, my friends.

We stand and watch for him to make his way through the crowd to us. He's spotted us and waves, makes his way. I want to cry so badly but hold back the throat ache, not wanting him to think I'm upset and knowing if I cry I can't see the expression on his face, "read" him, and that I will fall off the bleachers. I give him a first hug, sharing him with his sister. His dad extends hand, man to man. Eric's very somber and serious. We take a few family pictures and then he starts introducing us to new friends and his petty officers. Clowning, he and his friend, Rodriguez, pull their Navy raincoats off to show their new stripes as we click cameras. He shakes hands and congratulates others and receives it in return. More pictures.

Chief Petty Officer teases him about getting in trouble eating his food while standing in line. Then he says, "You only had to tell this recruit one time. You did a good job raising him. You can tell."

We go off to the rented car and ask him what he'd like to do first, and after eight weeks he can't think of a thing he'd like to do other than get away from the base. We do. Every time I look at him I have to remind myself to make each minute count. Store each memory until next we meet. During the day, we see just how much growing up he's done. Not only has he ironed all of his own clothes, "It's my life now," he says about ironing his clothes and underwear, but he gets up at one and two in the morning to help struggling recruits in his section iron. It's amusing at lunch to notice how carefully and fastidiously he eats. Crumbs are carefully wiped away from the plate. Periodically, the large hand runs down his front, smoothing his tie. We hear many stories but respect the things he cannot tell. "I signed a pledge to not reveal anything about battle stations," he says. We respect that and ask questions on other aspects of his eight weeks.

Later we see a movie, then head back to the Navy Lodge, together as a family. We look at the pictures we've taken all day. It almost feels like a family trip we're in the middle of taking. All too soon it's time for him to go back, early evening. Curfew. We drive through the iron gates, past the security station and deliver him back to the Navy. "I love you, Eric," his dad and I say for the final time that day. "Love you," says his sister, Jillian. "Love you all, too. Love you, Mom," he says with a peck on the cheek and a shoulder squeeze.

He slides out of the rental car, and we see him greet friends that are also being dropped off and watch them head off together, back to their ship. In step. We know we'll get to see him tomorrow.

When he's no longer in sight, we drive home to the Navy Lodge. And I try not to think too hard or too often about the ribbon pinned to his breast pocket.

FROM HERE TO THERE AND BACK AGAIN
(Eight Poems Compiled During the Journey)
by Jim Carlton

1.

Back Home from Vietnam
He came home from Vietnam, his body unscathed,
wishing to put the haunting memories of the war far away,
letting his hair grow long, his face unshaved,
when he came home to America where he would stay.

He searched and searched for the welcome home bands,
looked even harder for friends who had refused to go,
and all he could see was the blood on his hands,
plus, the terrified faces of his comrades dying in a row.

He didn't realize it would be so hard fighting in Vietnam,
figuring he'd get used to death, suffering and strife,
reckoned he'd be able to forgive and forget some,
just as soon as he returned to settle back into his civilian life.

He's been home from Vietnam now for 50-plus years,
went to college, had a successful career with his degree,
retired from working now, he still awakens with terrible fears,
and visions of blood, death and not really being set free.

2.

A Few More Steps

Just a few more steps down the road
when the light will turn to darkness,
or perhaps just the opposite, the
dark will be absorbed by the light.

A light which might guide me into
eternity and peace, away from this earth,
where I've seen and experienced
too much pain, sorrow and weeping.

This world has often seemed hostile
although it has shown me beauty
in mountains, on the plains
and the other side of far-reaching seas.

Destruction has reigned even inside
this beauty as fire thundered from the sky
melting forests into charred, scarred
nothingness or bits of rubble at best.
Even clouds have gushed out too much water,
causing streams and rivers to overflow,
turning the beauty into nothing again
as mud has covered the cities humans built.

The blue sea has turned red by blood flowing like rivers
from wounds inflicted by brothers and sisters
who claim they must make this pain by some holy
dictate or ideology given by a god only to a chosen few.

3.

Fear in Silence

Three in the morning
awakened groggy and
frightened unable to determine
what aroused me from sleep.

Bedroom pitch dark
with no street light outside
projecting its faithful
rays through my window.

No soft orange glow
from the numbers on
the digital clock perched
on the night stand by the bed.

No glimmer from the night light
in the darkened hallway which was
always faithful in the past
to lead me safely in the night.

As my brain transitioned
from its sleep-induced fog
it became apparent the
electric power was out.

It was not noise that had
startled me from sleep this
early morning but silence
had been the culprit.

Startling silence as if someone
had fired a gun near my ear
reflecting the confused
condition humankind was in.

Silence may have been therapeutic
to troubled minds in the past
was now frightening and unacceptable
in the modern human's life

4.

A Journey of Circles
It's been a journey of circles,
full of false starts, mysterious
moments in time, filled with
surprising beginnings and endings.

I still can't fully comprehend
its purpose, especially my part in it,
often, it seemed, only as an extra in
someone or something else's drama.

One tiny character in a cast of billions,
like in an epic war movie scene
with one or two main stand outs amongst
the countless fighting and dying warriors.

In the end, accolades heaped on
a handful of heroes receiving
honors for all the sweat and blood
shed by the extras noticed no longer.

5.
Smothering to Death
I don't really remember it,
not as a vision or anything like that.
It's just a feeling in there somewhere
deep down at the very core of me.

It tells me I've been many things,
at various times in numerous places on this earth.
I've sailed the seven seas as a pirate on a ship,
pilfering and taking just for the adventure of it.

I was a soldier, a sailor, a tailor, a store clerk,
a priest needing souls to help, a sinner seeking a priest.
I've killed and destroyed in one time, yet elsewhere
brought new life into this world as a mother in pain.

And the last time I died on this earth was at Pearl Harbor,
in 1941 entombed in the bowels of the USS Arizona.
This haunting memory sometimes still awakens me
in the night by a nightmare of slowly smothering to death.

6.
Chasing Shadows I
Chasing shadows
looking for light,
just a single
glimmering ray.

The shadows never
remain the same,
always moving and
changing shape.

Long one time but
next time short,
sometimes don't
even exist at all.

What remains are shadows
that don't mean a thing,
but I chase them nonetheless
because that's all I'm left with.

Chasing Shadows II
The form is not clear
in the shadows,
more a glob of nothing
than anything else.

It was evil I knew for sure
because had it been otherwise,
I'd have understood it and
not been afraid of the dark.

7.

The Stranger's Eyes
He connected only an instant,
wondering if it was just the
haunting look in her dark blue eyes
that attracted him to her.

Maybe it was the inexplicable,
the something beyond her eyes
and beyond even her body
he thought he recognized.

As if he had met her somewhere before,
perhaps they'd known each other
intimately in a different world or
even maybe even a far-away planet.

He felt a desire to embrace her,
as he might a newly found lost love
or just a casual friend,
who'd been away a long time.

As she turned to walk away,
their eyes meet again for an instant
and he was certain he knew her
so he thought he might speak.
She turned around abruptly,
her back now toward him and
no blue eyes to connect with this time
as she walked away rapidly.

Then as if suddenly awakened from deep sleep,
he realized he did not know her when
she moved further and further away and
blended into the crowd at the San Francisco Airport.

8.

Full Circle

He's come full circle to meet himself
in a place where it's impossible to really know
if it's the end or merely somewhere to begin anew,
for in many ways it feels both places are the same.

No memory remains of when he was born,
whether he really came from his mother's womb
or just stepped into his body to use it as a teaching aid,
to put away when the lesson is learned.

He's lived now for more than half a century,
and all that remains are fading memories
which sometimes seem more like dreams than reality,
if the difference can be distinguished between the two.

His mind searches for something to hold onto,
but it's impossible to grasp illusions because
they're so slippery and usually point to the words
which are spewed from the mouths of those who don't know.

Yes, he's come full circle to meet himself,
in a space where it's impossible to really know
whether it's the end or merely somewhere to begin again,
for it seems in many ways that both places are the same.

AMERICAN DREAM

(First Published in Torch Magazine *Fall 2015)*
by Steven DeLair

Dear Optimist and Pessimist,

While you were making your profound, eloquent and expansive arguments concerning the proverbial glass of water—I drank it.

Sincerely,

The Opportunist

The hope for a better tomorrow has no doubt been with the human race for thousands of years, but for a very long time that hope, for the most part, remained dim as the battle for survival dominated life. Deep contemplation of the future did not enter the mind's eye until much later in our history, when existence and the thought of it could include consideration of a possible improvement of life itself. From this perspective, the concept of a future being better than a present is relatively new.

The quality of life did slowly improve over the centuries, but not until America's founding was there such a radical and formal proclamation as "all men are created equal" and "endowed by their Creator with certain inalienable Rights, that among these are Life, Liberty and the pursuit of Happiness." That this proclamation was later acted upon, at the risk of life and treasure by an intellectual and social elite, and subsequently written into law, was as improbable as it was courageous.

This founding in freedom, with the rule and force of law, enabling average citizens to pursue a self-defined process to improve their condition in life, was a concept of startling world significance. That it was not at first understood to apply to all people does not diminish the importance of the lawful pursuit of happiness being established as a God given right.

Throughout the years after our founding, the "American dream" became a part of a national ethos, with varying definitions. The phrase entered the popular lexicon in *The Epic of America,* by historian James Truslow Adams: "It is not a dream of motorcars and high wages merely, but a dream of social order in which each man and each woman shall be able to attain to the fullest stature of which they are innately capable, and be recognized by others for what they are, regardless of fortuitous circumstances of birth or position."

Deep contemplation of the future did not enter the mind's eye until much later in our history, when existence and the thought of it could include consideration of a possible improvement of life itself.

Concerning those circumstances of birth, in 1963 a very courageous young leader and advocate for millions of those who were excluded from our nation's founding wrote the following in his "Letter from a Birmingham Jail": "We will win our freedom because the sacred heritage of our nation and the eternal will of God are embodied in our echoing demands. [...] When these disinherited children of God sat down at lunch counters they were in reality standing up for what is best in the American dream and for the most sacred values in our Judeo-Christian heritage, thereby bringing our nation back to those great wells of democracy which were dug deep by the founding fathers in their formulation of the Constitution and the Declaration of Independence" (King 301-02).

The 1790 U.S. Census counted 3,893,635 as the total population of the U.S. and its territory. Of that number, 694,280 were slaves—almost 18% of the population.

Dr. King's reference to the "most sacred values in our Judeo-Christian heritage" was one of the subjects of an address made by the famed Russian writer Alexander Solzhenitsyn at Harvard University in the summer of 1978. In his address entitled "A World Split Apart," Solzhenitsyn said, "The constant desire to have still more things and a still better life and the struggle to obtain them imprints many western faces with worry and even depression. The majority of people have been granted well-being to an extent their fathers and grandfathers could not even dream about." He continued, "Today, well-being in the life of Western society has begun to reveal its pernicious mask."

Solzhenitsyn was not a critic of the West. He was a critic of what he viewed as our weakness: the abandonment of the spiritual and religious foundation that made the West great. Writer Adam Gopnik characterized it as "incomes go up, steeples go down."

In contrast, Professor of Sociology Sandra Hanson and public opinion pollster John Zogby have reported that numerous public opinion polls taken from the 1980s to 2010 indicate that the majority of Americans feel that the American dream for their family is more about spiritual happiness than material goods.

The past thirty years of ever- increasing globalization combined with the recent destructive recession have contributed to a growing ambivalence concerning the American dream. Optimism about the future has historically been strong in the U. S., especially during the post-war decades from 1945 to 1975. America's relatively small sacrifice compared to the other combatants in World War II lifted our country out of the great depression and set the stage for U.S. world hegemony. The post-war economic boom engendered prosperity beyond our ancestor's comprehension, as noted by Solzhenitsyn. With our industrial capacity and infrastructure intact, post-war America resumed its growth and prosperity while the rest of the industrial world, with a few exceptions, was in the process of regaining their senses. The victory in World War II and the subsequent years of prosperity blurred our optimism with rising expectations that were not always rational.

America's relatively small sacrifice compared to the other combatants in World War II lifted our country out of the great depression and set the stage for U.S. world hegemony.

The U.S. has always been a trading nation, but the expansion of trade after the war increased to historic levels. Economists usually refer to globalization as the international integration in commodity, capital and labor markets. Globalization is not new, but the size and scope combined with the export of capital and technology is new.1 Economically, there have been major positive developments in the world because of expanded world trade. "Ironically, it is the very improvement in the economic well-being of hundreds of millions of people that raised the world's consciousness about poverty and inequality" said Robert Lerman of the Urban Institute. "The growing world recognition of massive disparities between rich and poor does not necessarily mean that economic inequality is worsening or that poverty is spreading." He also notes, "until a few hundred years ago, almost everyone experienced material poverty." Dr. Lerman refers to the studies of Columbia University professor Xavier Sala-I-Martin and his comprehensive 2002 analysis, which states, "the share of the world's population in severe poverty declined by two-thirds between 1970 and 1998. Even though the world population grew by

1.5 billion between 1980 and 1998, the number experiencing severe poverty declined by 160 million."

Bill Gates, speaking on behalf of The Bill and Melinda Gates Foundation, told an interviewer that it is a myth that world poverty is out of control. The severe poverty rate is lower than any time in history.

Somewhat against the grain of the preceding, mostly positive, analysis is Pope Francis's "Joy of the Gospel," which was published in November 2013. This Papal exhortation consists of five chapters and 51,000 words; a small part of it is devoted to the new global economic paradigm of growth and consumption.

Humanity is experiencing a turning point in its history as we see from the advances being made in so many fields. We can only praise the steps being taken to improve people's welfare in areas such as healthcare, education and communications. At the same time, we have to remember that the majorities of our contemporaries are barely living from day to day, with dire consequences. A number of diseases are spreading. The hearts of many people are gripped by fear and desperation, even in the so-called rich countries. [...] To sustain a lifestyle which excludes others, or to sustain enthusiasm for that selfish ideal, a globalization of indifference has developed. (44)

The Pope also uses the term "spiritual desertification" to describe the process of trying to build a society void of God, with the subsequent elimination of our Christian roots. This passage is only one piece of the Pope's theologically driven opinion of the global era, but it is representative of his views on this subject.

In April of 2012, June Zaccone, Professor of Economics (Emerita) at Hofstra University, presented a paper at Columbia University in response to the prevailing economic wisdom and in particular to Michael Spence, the 2001 Nobel Prize winner in Economic Science. (Spence's article "The Impact of Globalization on Income and Employment" typifies the influential positive analysis of the global era.) Professor Zaccone writes:

The mainstream view of globalization is that it is good for just about everyone—economies rich and poor grow faster and the incomes of workers everywhere rise faster. There may be a slight exception permitted for unskilled workers, but their problem is they need training. In any case, there is nothing to be done against the forces driving globalization. It is described as a natural market evolution, created by new technologies and better techniques permitting the effective management of far-flung operations. The reality is quite different. Technology has permitted globalization, which has been furthered by governments, especially ours, pursuing a corporate agenda. In the U. S., growth has slowed, worker's incomes have stagnated, inequality has risen to Gilded Age levels and the middle class has been splintered as jobs have disappeared. A few have joined top income levels, with far more pushed down to lower-skill, lower-wage service jobs.

Income inequality comes from the top extreme high income group and is not strongly associated with intergenerational mobility in the U.S.

The major concern of her paper is the harm done to the U.S. economy and its workers during the global era; nor is she convinced that workers in poor countries as a whole have benefited to the degree touted by the mainstream. She notes that the U.S. Census has projected that people of color, which includes Asians and Native Americans, will be the majority by 2042. She asks a very important question: "what will the economic and social prospects be then, if we don't improve their life chances?"

Expanding technology and the outsourcing of jobs have been the predominant sources of American job loss. Varying degrees of fear and anxiety about the future are widespread in the U.S. Many Americans sense that we are losing our ability to control our own destiny. Our politically polarized society gives rise to intransigence in Washington D. C. Income inequality and economic mobility are the subject of much debate.

Despite this debate, Greg Shaw and Laura Goffey, writing in *Public Opinion Quarterly,* state that "an examination of polls focused on inequality, taxes and mobility conducted between 1990 and 2011 reveals that American public opinion has remained fairly stable on these issues, despite changing political and economic conditions. There has been no dramatic shift of public opinion on these issues. Economic inequality, the government's role of redistribution, and taxation policies will likely remain divisive political issues in coming years in light of no public opinion on how to address growing economic inequality."

Is economic or social mobility declining in the U.S. as compared to other Western countries? In a National Bureau of Economics Research Study, "new evidence suggests that intergenerational mobility is fairly stable overtime in each of the nine census divisions of the United States even though they have very different levels of mobility." The rungs of the economic ladder have grown further apart, which represents increased inequality, but children's chances of climbing from lower to higher rungs have not changed. Income inequality comes from the top extreme high income group and is not strongly associated with intergenerational mobility in the U.S. "In light of the finding in our companion paper on the geography of mobility," the authors state, "the key issue is not that prospects for upward mobility are declining but rather that some regions of the U.S. persistently offer less mobility than most other developed countries" (Chetty).

A more provocative view by professor of economics and author Gregory Clark was featured in a recent *New York Times* article. Professor Clark believes that "the compulsion to strive, the talent to prosper and the ability to overcome failure are strongly inherited." In addition, "alternative explanations that are in vogue— cultural traits, family economic resources, social networks—don't hold up to scrutiny." In a *Mother Jones* magazine interview, Clark said, "modern societies haven't managed to increase social mobility above what it was in pre-industrial societies" (Harkinson). In his book *The Son Also Rises: Surnames and the History of Social Mobility,* Professor Clark details his creative and original methods of research using surname history in a diverse group of countries that predicted a high correlation of status across generations. If his analysis is only partially correct, it further complicates the debate over whether governmental policy should aim to help ameliorate life's inherent unfairness, which, if Clark is correct, begins at birth.

The global era has been scrutinized by many credible economists and others who, not surprisingly, come to different conclusions about the effects of this new world economic paradigm. The global era is complicated, and the analysis of information concerning it reflects that complexity. Despite the diversity of thought, there is sufficient understanding and knowledge to support the argument that for the greater world of developing and poor countries, with some exceptions, the economic gains in the global era have been dramatic. We are living in a profoundly historic era in regard to hundreds of millions of people who are no longer in severe poverty. Whether his improvement is sustainable over the long-term is yet to be seen.

For the U. S., the global era has been a winner for the corporate sector and obviously for millions of their shareholders. We can also acknowledge that everyone generally pays less for goods and services. The losers are the unemployed, underemployed, and those affected by wage stagnation. The social cost of disrupted lives, including government spending to lessen the negative effects of those losses, is not easy to calculate.

The fact that a modern competitive culture is increasingly populated by seriously dysfunctional, truncated families at the very time when a relatively healthy family structure is at the apex of need portends a future unlike anything witness in American history.

Despite these negatives (which are considerable), the preponderance of evidence, including our shared cultural capital and dynamism, point to an American dream that is shaken but alive and well. However, some of our largest social problems may have an increasing and profoundly negative impact on the future viability of the collective American dream that is inclusive of all people.

On January 8, 1964, President Johnson declared the War on Poverty. The current poverty rate according to the U.S. Census is about 15%, compared to 17.3% in 1965. The population of the U.S. has increased by approximately 122 million since 1965, however, so even at this slightly lowered rate, the total number of poor people in the U.S. is now 46.5 million, which equates to the total population of Spain. For those individuals and families who work hard and are prepared to meet the challenges of the 21st century, the dream for a good life is realistic. For those who are not prepared, the dream, if there is one, is probably wishful thinking.

Today, there are 24 million children living in fatherless homes. Almost half of all children in America are growing up in poverty, according to the U.S. Census. Out-of-wedlock births to mothers under age 30 are now over 50%. The negative social ramifications of these statistics are well known and documented. Our growing underclass is not prepared for the demands of the modern global world. The complexity of this problem defies any and all simple remedies. The fact that a modern competitive culture is increasingly populated by seriously dysfunctional, truncated families at the very time when a relatively healthy family structure is at the apex of need portends a future unlike anything witnessed in American history.

Is it possible for a modern wealthy nation in the global era to successfully coexist with increasing numbers of its population who are disconnected from its institutions and cultural ethos? In the Pope's previously mentioned exhortation, he says, "the family is experiencing a profound cultural crisis as are all communities and social bonds." He calls the family "the fundamental cell of society" and asserts, "the indispensable contribution of marriage to society transcends the feelings and momentary needs of the couple."

Do we have the collective ability to focus national attention to this or any other large problem? Do we have the will, the time or even a forum to contemplate and discuss these issues without our ubiquitous ideological blinders? Unfortunately, there is a dark side to the information age and our constant connectivity to an ever-expanding stream of diffused communication media. Some call it information overload.

Are we able to decipher the big picture of our individual and collective lives in the context of history and our present reality?

Perhaps Maggie Jackson said it best in her book *Distracted.*

Heads down, we are allowing ourselves to be ever-more-entranced by the unsifted trivia of life. With splintered focus, we're cultivating a culture of distraction and detachment. We are eroding attention—the most crucial building block of wisdom, memory and ultimately the key to societal progress. In attention, we find the powers of selection and focus we so badly need in order to carve knowledge from the vast, shifting and ebbing oceans of information. (235)

Is wisdom still relevant in contemporary America? Are we enamored by the "smart" and facile agility to navigate in the moment, with little knowledge or value of the past without thought beyond the immediate future? Are we capable of separating the important information from the trivial or irrelevant? Are we able to decipher the big picture of our individual and collective lives in the context of history and our present reality? If we can, do we have the wisdom to construct long-term goals and solutions? Or, are we reconciled to the notion that it is perpetually the best of times and the worst of times?

The future of the American Dream lies in the answers to those questions.

Notes by author:

Many people have the mistaken view that the increase of world trade, or globalization as now commonly refer to it, was purely a capitalist enrichment strategy. In fact, the recent impetus for this tremendous surge in world trade was the Atlantic Charter signed by President Roosevelt and British Prime Minister Winston Churchill in August of 1941. This charter defined a post-war vision that included lower trade barriers, the advancement of global social welfare and economic cooperation. The lack of these things, many then thought, had been a major cause of the war. The Atlantic Charter was the catalyst for the establishment of the United Nations. Previous attempts to promote collective world security, such as the League of Nations, had not been successful, but could commerce and welfare succeed where democracy had failed?

Works Cited

Adams, James Truslow. *The Epic of America*. 1931. San Antonio: Simon Publications, 2001.

Chetty, Raj, Nathaniel Hendfen, Patrick Kline, Emmanural Saez, and Nicholas Tumer. "Is the United States Still a Land of Opportunity? Recent Trends in Intergenerational Mobility." National Bureau of Economic Research working paper 19844, January 2014.

Clark, Gregory. "How Your Ancestors Determine Your Social Status." *New York Times,* February 23, 2004.

Clark, Gregory, Yu Hao, Neil Cummins, and Daniel Diaz Videl. *The Son Also Rises: Surnames and History of Social Mobility.* Princeton: Princeton University Press, 2014.

Collins, Lois M., and Marjorie Cortez. "Why Dads Matter." *The Atlantic* online: February 23, 2014.

Gates, Bill. Interviewed by Charlie Ross, PPS, January 20, 2014.

Gopnik, Adam. "Bigger Than Phil: When Did Faith Start to Fade?" *New Yorker:* February 17, 2014.

Hanson, Sandra L., and John Zogby. "The Polls—Trends: Attitudes about the American Dream." *Public Opinion Quarterly 74:3* September 2010.

Harkinson, Josh. "Is Upward Mobility in America a Fantasy?" Interview with Gary Clark, Mother Jones, February 4, 2014.

Jackson, Maggie. *Distracted: The Erosion of Attention and the Coming Dark Age.* Amherst, N.Y.: Prometheus Books, 2009.

King, Jr., Martin Luther. *A Testament of Hope: The Essential Writings and Speeches of Martin Luther King Jr.* Edited by James Washington. NY: HarperOne, 2003.

Leman, Robert I. "Globalization and the Fight Against Poverty." Paper presented at the 8th European Forum, Berlin. "Europe in World Politis," Berlin, November 15-16, 2002. Urban Institute web archive.

Pope Francis. "Joy of the Gospel." Exhortation. November 2013.

Sala-l-Martin, Xavier. "The World Distribution of Income." Working paper 8933. IDEAS:Economic and Finance Research, ideas, repec.org. 2002

Shaw, Greg and Laura Goffey. "Economic Inequality, Taxes and Mobility: 1990-2011." *Public Opinion Quarterly 76.3* Summer 2012 576-96.

Solzheniysyn, Alexander. "A World Split Apart." 1978 Harvard Commencement Address. *American Rhetoric Speech Bank.* Web.

Spence, Michael. "The Impact of Globalization on Income and Employment: The Downside of Integrating Markets." *Foreign Affairs,* July/August 2011.

Zaccone, June. "Has Globalization Destroyed the American Middle Class?" Columbia Seminar on Full Employment, Social Welfare and Equity. www.njfac. org. April 2012.

PLYMOUTH ADVENTURE
Our 400 Mile Road Trip for a Hot Roast Beef Sandwich

by Raymond Bates

As an amateur family genealogist, it is documented on the maternal side of my family, a relationship to one of the founders at Plymouth Rock of the Mayflower fame. I am a descendant of Major William Bradford through his daughter, Mercy. But, that's as close to Plymouth, Massachusetts, as I have been, by ancestry, heritage, and history. The story of my Plymouth adventure I write here begins when I met my first love-to-be at a faith-based college. We were both older students as compared to those just coming out of high school, both military veterans. She was army and I had navy/marine background. She was a single parent, raising a six-year-old daughter when we first met. Today, she might have "tweeted" me, but this is "old school," early 70's. Instead, she "TWIRP-ed" me. That would be considered PC incorrect to say or do today. It stands for "The Woman Is Required to Pay." I can see the eyebrows raise and hear the muffled howls of today's PC crowd. But, that's how we first met. She asked me first. We dated that first year, then set the date to tie the knot. Oops! PC blooper again. Denotes bondage, no doubt!

As college students, we learned to be thrifty. I had to work my way through college and the G.I. Bill didn't cover all of the credit courses cost. No student loans or scholarships. Eight years to complete four years of schooling. I'm satisfied with my achievement.

We decided we would travel to Sioux Falls, South Dakota, and be married in the church my bride-to-be was best known in and familiar with. My family was just five hours south, from Nebraska. ROAD TRIP!

The four of us would leave and do the trip together, future bride and groom, Sally and Raymond, six-year-old daughter, Jaime, and bride's best friend and Maid of Honor, Pam B., in our Plymouth auto.

The first third of the trip would also include some sightseeing in Yellowstone National Park, overnight it in a motel in western Wyoming, and then on to Rapid City. There, in the second third of our journey, we would spend overnight with Sally's Aunt Hanna.

The following day, before resuming the final third of our journey to Sioux Falls, we would drive about twenty-six miles from Rapid City to Mt. Rushmore and see the historic faces. Then, we would finally, arrive at the place where the hot roast beef sandwich and the four-hundred-mile road trip come into play.

Before we left Idaho, where we began our journey, my multi-tasking bride-to-be, had heard on the radio (YES, the RADIO, before the internet and social media, old school still alive and well...) Anyway, Sally had heard that it was possible to cook a small roast on your car engine manifold if you were traveling at least a four-hundred-mile distance. Coincidentally, about the distance from Rapid City to Sioux Falls, S.D.! She wanted to try it. Why not? It sounded so bizarre, it had to work. According to the radio, preparation was the key.

Roast Beef A La Plymouth Engine

Ingredients/supplies:

1 4-5 pound, 1" thick beef roast

1-2 pkgs. Dry Onion Soup Mix

1 roll aluminum foil

1 metal clothes hanger

1 roll masking tape

Directions:

Roll out 12-18" aluminum foil.

Gently wash beef with water, leave whole, do not dry.

Mix and spread one pkg of soup mix evenly on one side of roast.

Turn over and repeat process.

Begin wrapping aluminum foil around meat--do not tear.

Secure with tape.

Repeat with second layer of foil and tape.

Bend hanger to make cradle to rest roast in.

Use tape to secure roast.

Roast will be placed touching mainfold of engine when cool.

Serves: 1 wedding party

The roast was put on the engine at Aunt Hannah's house in Rapid City and twenty-six miles later, at the Faces, you could already faintly smell roast beef. We popped the hood of the Plymouth, just to check that there was no major juice leaking from the meat. A couple, walking by, inquired and looked on in bewilderment at our set-up.

We visited Mt. Rushmore for a couple of hours and then we were off to Wall Drug, about a two-hundred-mile journey from Rapid City. We spent some time at Wall Drug, allowed the car engine to cool down, and then it was time to check the roast and possibly flip the sides. We did so, and you could see where the foil was beginning to scorch from the heat coming off the manifold. The old 1966 Plymouth was ideally made to hold the roast. Only time would tell if it was doing the job we hoped it was.

It was about 2:30 a.m. when we arrived at our destination in Sioux Falls. Everyone was glad to be out of the cramped car. Of course, Mother Clarke wanted to feed us. She was a bit surprised when we brought in our own "400 Mile Road Trip Roast." It came out great, as if it had been roasted in their kitchen oven! Hot roast beef sandwiches at 2:30 a.m. It was a delicious way to end a safe trip!

This was not the only time we tried and used this and other thrifty and frugal budget ideas during our years together as a family. We also branched out to hot dogs with the cigarette lighter, canned hams we punctured in advance, and many other delicious experiments (with mixed success). We prided ourselves on being modern day pioneers.

GOING UP UNDER A PARACHUTE

by Donald Dingman

There were no clouds in the sky above Ainsworth, Nebraska, that June day in 1976. I was one of three jumpers doing two demonstration jumps at the airport for an air show. I remember it well because I was going to make one of my most memorable parachute jumps, number 428.

The first jump was to show how we can travel, or 'track' in skydiver lingo, across the sky to reach another jumper in freefall. We left the airplane together and separated like a starburst.

Because of FFA flight rules, we couldn't take off for our second jump until all planes were back on the ground. We used this time to determine the order of exit. I would be the base jumper. The one who goes out first, and the one who watches the altitude to signal the others to break off and deploy their chutes.

We made our jump run at 7,500 feet for a thirty second freefall. The three of us would leave the aircraft a second or two apart, then track to catch the other two. We were smiling at each other when at 3,000 feet I made the signal. We broke hands and separated. At 2,500 feet, I pulled my ripcord to deploy my chute. I checked to see it was fully open before I grabbed the steering toggles. I glanced down at the altimeter on my front-mounted reserve chute and saw that I was almost a hundred feet above where I was when I pulled my ripcord. This is when I also realized that I was not going down. I was literally sitting in the sky and enjoying the scenery. Only a camera on a drone could be in a similar situation, but not in the silence I enjoyed.

I had opened in a thermal updraft. With my hands controlling the steering openings at just the right position, I was going there as long as it held. All of us were jumping with *Para-Commander* or PC style round canopies, the ultimate round canopy, until being replaced with the square wing styled chutes. This canopy took two and a half minutes to reach the ground at approximately a 45-degree angle.

I watched the two other jumpers float to the ground, gather their chutes, and walk to the packing area. All while I never changed altitude. I was just sitting there watching all of the goings on down on the ground for what seemed like five minutes. I then remembered the flight rules about the next act taking off, and let go of my toggles, starting my descent out of the updraft.

Now remember when I said all planes had to be down before another could go up? Well, the same goes for parachutists. After I was back on the ground, I was told that a regional air carrier had to circle the field until I was down. So I can claim that I also held up an airliner.

LISTEN TO THE WIND

by Tom Seib

The dust quietly rises from the buffalo wallow
and drifts slowly toward the north,
coating the stiff golden faces of sunflowers
bending in the breeze.

The wind never stops blowing in Western Kansas,
it only changes velocity and direction.
It invites man to contemplate, to meditate,
to listen; listen to the wind.

Listen to the wind as it ripples through the wheat fields
moving in golden waves across the prairie.

Listen to the wind as it carries a solitary, soaring hawk
in search of prey, on its currents.

Listen to the wind as an old windmill on a lonely,
deserted farmstead sings its melodious tune.

Listen to the wind as it rises and tugs a grizzled farmer's seed corn hat
and whips his wife's hair.

Listen to the wind as it pushes rain into faces
during a sudden thunder storm.

On the high plains of Kansas, the wind never stops,
it only moves in circles under a vast open sky,
rising and falling, but never ceasing its pull
on the hearts and minds of the itinerant souls who live there.

THE FINAL STORM

by Tom Seib

It started in the west as a faint whisper
on a hot June night, the clouds rolling
like smoke on high waves. The horses began
kicking at their stalls, their nostrils flaring.

It reminded me of Grandpa the night the barn blew down.
He said we would start again as he picked up the
twisted boards and piled them next to the gate.

There is the road he walked to check the crops every day.
They always sang for him, but I could never hear the tune.
Like the ladies in the front pew at church,
He would often kneel in the middle of the field, his head upturned.

Grandpa, his face reflected in the lamplight
as we huddled in the rancid storm cellar,
saw an old river baptism in the torrents of rain and wind.
All I saw was a scary storm.

At dawn we walked to the place he always knelt
and saw the bent heads of wheat like the final
moments at the graveside. When you take everything away, what's left?

A FEATHER MERCHANT'S TALE

(Feather Merchant: A derogatory term applied to support
troops by those in a combat role)
by William (Bill) Smutko

The chrome and Naugahyde chair in the lobby of the V. A. Med Center accepts my butt and back with ease and comfort; my body relaxes. It's near the elevators and the coffee aroma from the Starbucks counter to my right drifts over me.

Maybe I should get a cup.

I really look forward to these appointments. The staff is courteous and helpful. They are respectful almost to the point of overdoing it.

I'm waiting for an orderly to help me to the fourth floor for my 2:00 P.M. physical therapy appointment with Karl Freud. I commented on his name my first visit. Though I'm sure he'd heard it a thousand times, Karl smiled and acknowledged it.

My hands rest easily on the cane between my knees. There are two small L. E. D. flashlights taped to it. One is mounted high and at a slight angle out from the cane to illuminate out in front of me. The other is mounted low to light up where the cane is going so I won't put it down where it's not stable. The skin on the hands supported by the cane is almost transparent and covered with brown age spots and bruising from the blood thinners.

When did I get old?

Getting a cup of coffee and getting back into this chair with it, probably not a good idea.

As comfortable as I feel here, I'm sitting away from the others to avoid the anxiety of having to talk with them, especially the Vietnam Vets. But, I watch them while I wait.

There are a lot of guys here needing help. Like me.

The younger ones, my son's age, are veterans of Iraq and Afghanistan, the ones my age are Vietnam Vets, the older ones from the Korean War. You don't see WWII vets around anymore.

A young guy walks by with a titanium blade where his right foot and lower leg used to be. My right leg tingles in empathy.

Missing in action.

An incredibly obese fellow near my age with an obviously new amputation of his left foot is pushed by in a wheel chair.

Diabetes.

There are a lot of guys with bad teeth from lack of care. The ones in wheelchairs usually have, what I guess to be, a wife pushing. There are younger people escorting an ageing parent. I see a lot of young women.

A couple of Vets walk by wearing baseball caps proclaiming them to be Veterans of the Vietnam War.

There seem to be a lot of Marines.

Ya know, I've never seen anyone wearing a 9th Infantry Division patch or pin.

A guy about my age, but in better shape, walks over to the chair next to me. He has a ramrod straight back and a purposeful gait, turns around and sits down without having to grab the chair arm to balance himself.

I unconsciously lift my cane in front of my body.

Hope to hell he's not the chatty type.

I start shifting around in my chair to the side away from him.

He turns to me and says, "First visit. To get a baseline. You?"

Good manners outweigh my anxiety. I turn my head to the left and say, "This is the sixth since my stroke."

The other fellow sticks out his hand. "Mike Wilson," he says.

"Sid Galloway," I say, reaching across my body to shake the outstretched hand.

An orderly pushing a cart loaded with boxes walks by.

"What branch of the service were you?" Mike asks.

"Army," I say, twisting my watch around my wrist as I fight through my anxiety.

"Me too," says Mike. "What unit?

Talking to him is getting easier.

I stop fiddling with my watch. "709th Maintenance Battalion 9th Infantry Division."

A Vet in a wheelchair wearing a Vietnam Veteran's baseball cap with an 82nd Airborne pin rolls past.

"I'm 9th Division as well. 5th battalion 60th Infantry," says Mike. "Where were you stationed?"

I turn my body so I can see him better. "I was there for two years. Ben Luc for the first and Tan An for the second."

"When were you there?" asks Mike.

"November '68 through November '70," I say.

Mike leans closer and asks, "Were you in Ben Luc in March of '69?"

Why is he so excited about this?

I lean into him. "Yes. Why?"

A guy with an oxygen concentrator and labored breathing sits down behind us. He reeks of cigarette smoke.

"My platoon and I were in some of those Hueys that responded to the attack on your compound," says Mike.

A smile erupts across my face. "A sincere if much belated thanks!"

"For REMFs you guys seemed to have held your own," he says.

"It's amazing how determined you can become and how much of your combat training you remember when your life is on the line." *I haven't talked to anyone about Vietnam since I got back. Memories are spewing from me like infection from a lanced boil.*

"I lost a couple of friends killed, and several other friends and I were wounded in that attack." A couple of doctors walk past sipping from Starbucks cups and chatting.

"We took no casualties that night. They had all didi maued out of there after the artillery and Cobra gunships worked them over. Our job was to secure the area and do a body count," replied Mike.

"Where do you live?"

"Gretna. I retired from the Army after twenty and have been selling real estate since," replied Mike. "What about you?

"I have a small vineyard near Fremont."

"Time to go. I don't want to be late for the doctor." He heads off for the Blue Clinic.

An orderly shows up with a shiny new wheelchair and holds it steady. I rise from my seat with the help of my cane and turn around, reach back, grab the arms of the wheelchair and lower myself into it. The orderly wheels me over to the elevators and pushes the up button.

I let out an enormous pent up breath.

Why was I so anxious? That wasn't at all painful.

"Do we have time for me to get a cup of coffee?" I ask the guy pushing my chair.

Prelude to a Combat Zone

The green glow of the radium number on my watch show it's three A.M. The rough sheets smell of laundry detergent and bleach. I look through the dark at the ceiling, my mind an unending line of rail cars each filled with a different thought.

Where will the C. O. assign me?

How will the troops react to me?

Will the mechanics know their jobs? What will I do if they don't?

Will the Platoon Sergeant be a help or a hindrance? How will I work around him if I have to?

I flop over and bury my head under the thin pillow trying to find a place to get off.

How will I react in a combat situation? I hope to God I don't freeze or worse, run.

The telephone on the bedside table rings sending the train on to a siding. "It's six thirty Lieutenant Galloway," says the voice coming out of the handset. Time to get up and moving.

Drizzle and darkness shape the day as we board the bus. We track water from the street in with us.

Smells of wet people.

The rain picks up and drums a bleak tattoo on the roof of the vehicle as it wallows along toward the airport. There are no brass bands or young women throwing flowers and blowing kisses to see us off. There is a group of sodden protestors wielding waterlogged signs proclaiming, "Make Love not War," and, "Baby Killers."

The Douglas DC 8 has Saturn Airlines painted on the fuselage.

Appropriate. Feel like I'm going to another planet.

The rain escalates into a violent storm. Thunder from a close by lightning strike is as deafening as an 8-inch cannon report and the rain ricochets off the fuselage like automatic weapons fire. My seat is between two captains. It's cramped, no movies, no pillows and the smell of apprehension is thick. I sit down, wide eyed and wired.

The Angst Express leaves the siding, thoughts keep rolling by. *Will there be enough spare parts? Three quarter ton truck starters were impossible to get at Ft. Benning.*

Potato Pancakes

I'm in the middle of a very large un-lighted metal building near the center of the Long Binh Army Depot. Truck starters surround me on the gray concrete floor, hundreds of them. I kick at one and throw up my hands in frustration.

These are for 5-ton trucks. I need starters for ¾-tons.

I've only been in country a month. But, it's my job to provide any parts needed, and ¾ ton starters are badly needed. I've been ordered by my company commander - he told me it was time I lost my cherry - to drive up here and find at least three of them. The Third Brigade is desperate for them. Three vehicles are dead-lined for the lack of one. Company, Battalion, Brigade and Division Commanders consider a dead-lined vehicle an abomination.

Hell, I was valedictorian of my class at Virginia Military Institute. I should be able to solve this problem.

Sergeant First Class Steven Kolodziejski is helping me with the problem. I've heard the rumors about him: that as a nineteen-year old, the judge gave him the option of enlisting or going to jail, that he has been promoted and demoted so many times his stripes have zippers on them, that he is part owner of the Palace Hotel, the best whore house in Saigon. They're just rumors.

I know for sure that he likes to be called Fix because Kolodziejski means something like repairman in Polish. I know that he arrived in Vietnam in December 1965 with the 1st Logistics Command and transferred to the 709th Maintenance Battalion in 1967 as the Non-Commissioned Officer in Charge of the Battalion's Expediter Detachment here at the Long Binh Army Depot.

He has been at the depot in one capacity or another since his arrival in country four years ago. He knows it better than the troops now assigned to run it. Fix finds parts no one else can. And, he was awarded the Distinguished Service Cross, second only to the Medal of Honor, for his bravery during the Tet Offensive. He's a legend in the 709th.

Fix and I are looking into every possible storage location and cubby hole where starters might have been misplaced. I've already looked at the jeep starters with no luck. I checked the locations for 2 ½-ton, ¾-ton and jeep alternators hoping a clerk didn't know the difference between a starter and an alternator. Not there. Fix has checked new shipments and talked with the expediter teams from the other divisions. He's even called the Navy and Air Force with no joy. Voices from near the door catch my attention. They're loud and heated. I walk quietly toward the entrance. A short stocky man in a South Korean Army uniform and a Specialist 6 are off in a dimly lit corner. They appear to be haggling over a wooden box with a red ball painted on it. The Specialist reluctantly hands over the box. The Korean's left arm passes through a shaft of sunlight from a hole in the roof as he hands the Specialist a wad of cash. I notice that he has a scorpion tattoo on the back of his left hand and that the box holds what looks like truck parts.

That soldier is selling parts, selling out the troops in the field. I don't want to believe it, but I saw it and can't un-see it. Even the army has guys who put their own wants first.

* * *

The Expediter Detachment's three room, shrapnel and bullet pitted hooch has a patio made of wooden pallets covered with miss-matched sheets of plywood. The razor wire perimeter is about twenty-five yards to the east of us. Fix and I are outside, sitting in the warm, late afternoon sun. I'm rocking back and forth in my chair twisting my watch around my wrist.

How do I tell Captain Black that I was unable to complete my mission?
I guess valedictorian doesn't carry much weight here.

Fix uses a church key to punch two holes in the tops of two cans of Schlitz and hands me one. He is getting ready to cook pork chops over charcoal on a home-made grill.

I rub the back of my neck and take a sip of my beer. "If you had a grater, a couple of potatoes, an onion, some flour, and an egg or two I could make some potato pancakes to go with those."

"Fuckin' great idea. Potato pancakes. The army doesn't teach its fuckin' cooks how to make that stuff."

Fix finds an empty three-pound coffee can, a hammer and a large nail. He starts punching even rows of holes into the side of the can at an angle so the rough edges form many cutting surfaces. It is crude but it should work.

I start grating potatoes.

I can't believe that guy was actually stealing those parts.

"What was Tet like?" I ask, wanting to not think about failing my mission or the theft of parts.

"Somethin' else, the fuckin' NVA started with a mortar barrage. Cooks, clerks, forklift drivers, truck drivers, everbody, crouched down along the perimeter and waited it out. The mortars wounded a few guys but didn't do any real damage. Then the cock suckers charged. We opened fuckin' fire when they were about one hundred yards out and kept firing. Stopped them at the fuckin' wire. When it was over there were sixty fuckin' bodies stacked up in front of us. Some of the guys went down and took trophies. One guy thought he was a fuckin' bullfighter and took a couple of ears. We had some wounded on our part of the perimeter but, no one was killed."

"How much fuckin' flour are you putting in those, LT? You're not making potato bread!"

"These are Slovakian style like my mother's mother, my Baba, makes. Only a couple of tablespoons. It helps hold them together."

"My mother used to put caraway seeds in them too," Fix says.

"I wish we had some. I take another slug from my beer. "That and some sauerkraut."

"Can't help with the sauerkraut but, kim chi is a lot like it, and that I can get. Now that I think about it, I'm going to call an old friend."

My guts are shaking as I ladle scoops of grated potato pancake batter onto the griddle on the Coleman gasoline fired camp stove.

"Have you made enough potato pancakes for one more?" asks Fix. "I've invited Mr. Ryu Mal-Chin, a South Korean Warrant Officer, to dinner. He's bringing the kim chi."

"Yes but, you won't have any left over for lunch tomorrow."

"Not a problem, want another beer?"

I reply in the affirmative. Fix punches holes in the tops of two more Schlitz cans and hands me one and starts laying pork chops on the grill over the hot coals.

I dread telling Captain Black I couldn't find the starters.

I use a spatula and lift the done pancakes off the griddle and ladle on a four more. A few minutes later Fix turns the six pork chops over to cook on the other side. He uses a fork to move the pork chops to a plate and takes them inside the hooch. I follow with the potato pancakes.

I take a drink from my Schlitz. *The pork chops and potato pancakes sure smell good. Even the smell of them makes the beer taste better. But, I'm not hungry.*

Fix gets up to answer a knock on the door. A short, broad shouldered man wearing a South Korean Army uniform and a wide friendly grin is standing on the threshold holding a wooden box in front of him. "Welcome my friend," he says, clapping him on the shoulder. "Lieutenant, this is Mr. Ryu. Mr. Ryu, this is Lieutenant Galloway. Mr. Ryu has brought some presents."

The Korean strides into the hooch and sets the box on the table. I see the red ball, painted on the side. As he puts the box down, I see the tattoo of a scorpion on the back of his left hand. *That was the hand that paid for the stolen parts.*

"After dinner we'll go into Saigon and spend the night at the Palace, the beds are much more comfortable. Oh, and the starters will cost you a Rolex," says Fix.

Ben Luc

Ben Luc is a village of about a thousand farmers and shop keepers. It's an amalgamation of white stucco buildings with burnt orange tile roofs and shanties made of old packing crates with dirt floors. There are no lawns. There are vegetable gardens and pens populated with the ever-present white ducks and black pigs. Venders sell gasoline in glass liter bottles to families of four on Honda 90 motor bikes. Short, thin, brown men constantly smoking, squat with their behinds and feet firmly on the ground. They market clothing on tables and pineapples on carts next to highway 1A the Main Supply Route between Long Binh and Dong Tam. Shirtless, thin, brown boys herd water buffalo on the edge of the village. Black-clad farmers in conical straw hats are doubled over in the paddies tending the young rice plants in the green paddies surrounding the village.

Ben Luc, the military post, a compound about 200 yards across, is adjacent to Ben Luc the village. It is a collection of olive drab tents, olive drab trucks and trailers, olive drab shipping containers "connexes," olive drab sandbags and black Mekong Delta dirt / mud. It smells of diesel exhaust, dust and mold. The shop areas and mess hall are in tents. The parts storage is in the trailers. Everyone lives in sandbag-sided squad tents which feel more like WWI dugouts. Company headquarters and the "bomb shelter" are sandbag covered connexes. The compound is in a secure area but, it still has a defensive perimeter. We are surrounded by miles of rice paddies easily traversed by the Viet Cong. A ring of thirty sand-bag rimmed fox holes behind concertina wire and claymore mines surrounds the outpost. Each platoon has an area of responsibility and every person is assigned a firing position.

Life is monotonous, cloistered, almost monastic. The day for the sixty of us is regimented with scratchy bugle calls broadcast through olive drab loudspeakers. The sound of *First Call* wakes us to a day indistinguishable from the one before. We do the same job as yesterday and tomorrow. We work with, eat with and smell the same people. A visitor from another unit is a welcome change. The scenery never changes, the same workplace, the same mess hall, the same sleeping quarters. The purpose of the perimeter has become blurred. Is it to keep the enemy out or us in?

The monsoon rains have pushed water in from the rice paddies, filling the ditch that runs through a culvert under our front gate.

"Fifteen two, fifteen four and a pair is six," Pete Lawson says as he pegs. "We should get a couple of bamboo poles and fish the ditch, it comes from the river through the rice paddies. It would be a diversion from the monotony, and the feeling of being imprisoned by the perimeter. And, it would help my sanity. Damn it Sid! I miss fly fishing for trout."

"So do I," I say. "The cold, clear water pulling at your waders; the screech of a king fisher as it flies down the river; The clean fresh smell of the trees and grass; the Zen-like rhythm of casting; the song the line sings as it whispers through the guides. I miss it all."

I give our hooch girl money to buy Pete and me each a bamboo fishing pole. He and I build a pier of wooden pallets near the gate out to the water. We use raw bacon from the mess hall to bait our hooks. "When I was a kid my brother and I used to use this to catch crawdads," I tell him as we put the baited hooks into the muddy water. It's a diversion, much like the weekly movie night. I enjoy the fight of a fish on the end of a line, but there's no music. We manage to catch several large, what look like catfish, which we give to the girl.

* * *

It's early afternoon on a warm day in early March. The Company Commander has called for all the officers and senior NCOs to meet him in the mess hall. In the tent along with the C O is the Battalion's S-2, intelligence and security officer.

"Division has information from one of their prisoners of war that a large Viet Cong force is going to attack one of the outlying units," The S-2 says. "It is to happen sometime in the next week to ten days. Ben Luc is in a supposedly secure area, but it's surrounded by miles of rice paddies that are empty at night. The Battalion Commander wants to make sure that you are prepared for any attack that might come. There is a platoon of Cobra Gunships and two air mobile infantry companies ready at Tan An Airfield seven miles away. They will respond when needed."

* * *

We open our eyes wider and pay more attention to what is going on around us. We aren't combat troops and everyone's anxious. The guard is doubled at night and we sleep with our boots on and our weapons and ammunition close at hand.

It's sundown on the 17th of March and I'm Officer of the Guard. In the tropics it gets dark quickly. There is no lingering dusk. It goes from sundown to dark in a few minutes. When that dark comes with no moon, it is almost as dark as being one hundred feet into an un-lighted coal mine.

I look into the surrounding emptiness and imagine 200 individual Viet Cong trickling out of their villages, filtering through the miles of rice paddies like water under a sliver of moon. They have brought the weapons of assault with them. They have light mortars to open holes in the razor wire. There are RPGs to knock out hard targets and 180 of the omnipresent 7.62mm AK-47 assault rifles.

My view through the Starlight Scope shows movement about a 150 yards out from the wire. A second look and I see people carrying weapons. I crank the handle on the field phone and ask for the C. O. "We have V.C. at on150 yards and moving in."

"Send up parachute flares and open fire," he says.

The sound of our gunfire brings the others to their fox holes and they begin firing on the attacking V.C.

Viet Cong mortar shells start landing in the wire, working their way toward our firing positions. RPGs explode in the compound, blowing up parked vehicles and setting tents on fire. Snapping all around are 7.62 mm bullets. Two carom off my helmet; another creases my flak jacket just over my right kidney. The intense sound from 400 hundred automatic rifles, machine guns, exploding mortar shells and RPGs is making my ears bleed.

My platoon is under heavy pressure. Tom Payne, one of my supply clerks is shredded by an RPG, and I see a furrow plowed across SP4 Rogers' upper left arm.

The light produced by muzzle flashes, exploding shells and RPGs is strobe-like and surreal.

I'm directing the platoon's fire and seeing that everyone has ammunition. I have four bandoliers of M-16 ammunition in my left hand and my M1911 Colt .45 cal. automatic in my right as I work my way to my Platoon Sergeant's position on my left. Two Viet Cong run out in front of me. I react without thinking and put a .45 cal. round in the chest of each before they can fire. The V. C. are close enough to me that arterial blood from the second splatters my right hand and face.

The smell of burnt gunpowder and blood saturates my sense of smell. Shrapnel from an RPG rips through my right thigh and I go down.

Friendly artillery fire and gunships from Tan An drive off the remaining Viet Cong. The battle only lasts thirty minutes. Twenty other members of "C" company and I are medevac'd to the Division hospital at Dong Tam.

Last Man Fallen

There were no phone calls to return, no reports to fill out, nothing to do at our desks so we came to the Officers' club. I've been drinking beer since nine a.m. and am almost euphoric. There is nothing for us to do because we're going home. Our unit, the 3rd Brigade of the 9th Infantry Division, has stood down. We have survived our time in harm's way. In two days, we'll climb on board an airplane that will return us to the land of Big Macs, Kentucky Fried Chicken and pizza by the slice. There will be no more mortar or RPG attacks or being as much imprisoned as protected by the perimeter's razor wire and claymore mines.

Five of us, Tom Hansen, the Air Cushion Vehicle Squadron Commander: Steve Rodgers, the Brigade logistics Officer: Jim Futa, assistant Brigade logistics officer; Hank Gunther, an infantry Platoon Leader, and me, the other Assistant Logistics Officers decide to play poker for something to do. We're a bit unsteady as we move our beer cans and bodies from the bar to a table and sit down. It is one in the afternoon on a Tuesday.

"Gentlemen, before we get started," Hank Gunther says slurring his words a little, "I feel the need to warn you that I was voted the luckiest cadet in my class at Wentworth Military Academy."

"Why?" Hansen asks. He lights a camel and gulps from one of the open cans of Miller High Life in front of him.

"I'm gifted, I guess. Luck follows me everywhere." Gunther glances around the table. "My senior year at Wentworth, when I was home for Christmas, I hit some black ice at sixty miles an hour. The car rolled four times. I walked away with a slightly sprained wrist. The car was totaled. It scared the shit out of me. But what a rush. I loved it."

"You're still Mister Lucky. I heard you cheated death, again. Two weeks ago. Your platoon flipped an ambush set for you," I say.

"Another rush," Gunther says. You could tell he was excited just thinking about it. "While on patrol we changed into an assault formation for practice. The gooks thought we had spotted their ambush and opened fire too soon. Body count, us - zero, gooks – 35. Fucking exhilarating. I get a hard-on just talking about it."

"Okay, Mister Lucky, let's test that luck," Rodgers says shuffling the cards. "Seven card Stud, High Chicago. A dime to play."

The cigarette and cigar smoke is almost a fog around the table and there is at least one open can of beer in front of each of us.

"Turned the ACVs over to ARVN this morning," Hansen says. He pushes his dime chip into the center of the table. "Happy to feel the weight of them off my shoulders."

"Wonder how long they'll last under ARVN maintenance," Futa says. He antes, then takes a long draw from his Pall Mall.

Rodgers finishes dealing two hole cards and one face up to each of us. "Jim, you're high card. Start the betting." He picks up his Cuesta Rey 898 cigar, takes a long drag on it. The aroma drifts above our heads.

Futa looks at his hole cards. "Nickel." He drops a white chip into the center and sips beer.

"I'm in," I say. I toss the chip to the pot, a Winston smoking in the ash tray next to me. Everybody calls.

Rodgers deals out the next five cards. "Tom, Jack of hearts, possible straight. Hank, four of hearts. Not so lucky, Mister lucky. Jim, five of spades, no help. Sid, ten of clubs possible straight. A five of clubs for me. Jim, your ace is still high card."

"Check," Futa says.

"Check."

"Same."

"I'll go with the flow," Hansen says. He drains his Miller High Life.

"Dime," Gunther says.

Five red chips make their way to the stack.

"Lady Luck sitting on your lap, is she Gunther?" asks Rodgers.

"And wiggling her ass against my pecker."

Rogers deals the next card to each player.

"I'm high, pair showing." I bet a dime and take a drag from the Winston in the ash tray. Rodgers and Hansen fold. Gunther raises a nickel and Futa flips a white chip onto the pile. I put in my nickel.

Rodgers deals the last card down to Gunther, Futa and me. "Sid, you're still high hand." "Dime to ya, Hank."

"Raise you a quarter." He chuckles and slides a red and a blue chip toward the pile in the center of the table.

"I'm out," Futa says. He empties his beer.

"Call," and I drop a blue chip on the pile. "What've ya got besides the high spade?"

"Captain Galloway, my jacks beat your tens and here is the king of spades," Gunther says. He flips over two of his hole cards.

"You are one lucky son-of-a-bitch," I say. "That jack was your last card. Maybe we shouldn't be playing cards with you after all."

Rodgers hands the cards, "Your deal."

Futa's folding chair clacks like castanets as he slides it back across the concrete floor. He sways a bit as he stands. "I'm going for another beer. Any of you short timers want one? What the hell, I'll just get a round," weaving slightly as he makes his way to the plywood bar.

I start shuffling the deck slowly and deliberately. Being half in the bag has slowed me down. "Five-card draw. Buy in's a dime."

Jim returns with five green and gold Miller High Life cans. The humidity condensing on them shines like an early morning frost. He passes the beers around and slides a red chip to join the four others in the center of the table.

I deal five cards to each player and say to Rodgers, "Your bet."

"A dime. When I get home, I'm playing thirty-six holes of golf every day for a week."

Everyone stays. "How many cards?" I ask. We all take three, except Gunther, who takes one.

"Trying to fill that straight, Mister Lucky?" I ask. "Your bet," I say to Rodgers.

"Dime again."

"Raise a dime. My wife already got tickets to the Packers, Bears game," Hansen shares as he pushes two red chips into the pot.

Gunther adds his chips to the pile, "Make it 30 cents."

"Guessing he filled that damn straight. So I'm out. I'm going to find the best restaurant in Baltimore and eat until I can't move," Futa says.

"Out. Don't think I can beat lucky boy," I interject. "There's a stretch of the South Platte River Just below Cheeseman Dam they call the Miracle Mile. The water is clear and cold and the trout get big as tunas. I'm going to fish there every day for a year."

"In," Rodgers says.

"I'm calling your bluff," and Hansen adds another dime.

"Read 'em an' weep. Seven high straight. Luck doesn't even begin to describe me. Wish I'd been here during Tet. It would have been one fucking long adrenaline high! Shit, I almost wish I weren't going home."

"You're not lucky, you're nuts," I reply, very glad I am going home.

We play eight more hands of poker and each of us buys a round of beer. Hank wins four of the eight, including the last one which he wins with two pair, aces and eights, the infamous dead-man's hand.

"Guess we're done here," Gunther smiles. "And just to show you guys how much I appreciate your company. I'm going to buy a round of Jim Beam with a beer chaser. Then I need to pack it in, I signed up for one last ride along with B troop tomorrow on an insertion."

"Mister Lucky," I say. "Just can't stand down from the rush."

Gunther laughs and waves to us as he heads to his hooch.

The next day, about noon, Rodgers calls Jim Futa and me to his office with the news, "Hank Gunther was killed this morning. The helicopter he was in was lifting off after unloading its troops when an RPG hit the doorframe right next to him. The chopper went down. Gunther was dead before it hit the ground."

THE CABIN
by Joel Elwell

I remember
the muddy water
of the river,
the leaves and cotton
it carried on its surface,
and the fish it carried beneath.

I remember
the tree blocked blue sky
above the river,
mysterious, dark and eerie
at night,
filtered and adventurous
during the day.

I remember
rowing the boat across the river
having the perfect game plan with my cousins,
screaming with fear and delight
during the battles,
and losing the mud ball fights to our older brothers.

I remember
the kitchen table
with that odd designed cloth
covering its abused surface,
standing near the sliding glass doors
with chairs that should've been broken
facing the river.

I remember
shooting fresh tin cans
with BB guns that seemed like rifles,
laughing at fireworks on my birthday
and flooding out the badger holes.

I remember
Uncle Bob,
his balding head, the smoke from
his cigarettes and his comforting
father-like smile.

I remember

Falling through the ice
Falling on the gravel
Running from big snakes
Hiding from tornadoes
And always taking shelter
In the cabin

THE STATION

by Mary Baker

She'll be coming under the mountain when she comes.
You can hear the shiny train rolling down the tracks,
click-clack, click-clack, just around the final bend.
You can't see her yet, but you know she is coming,
the pride of the Manhattan Main Line, the newest of the fleet,
taking people to and from work, their homes and their play.
And even though you can't see her yet, you know she is there.

Like when you see the shiny shopping cart full of blankets
and cardboard sitting at the end of your last stop.
You don't see the homeless person sitting behind the rubble, but you know she is
there too.
She and others like her are waiting for you and I to leave the underground,
and see what we have left behind for them.
Maybe something to eat, or a scarf or a glove; it's been a long-cold winter on the
East Coast this year.
And once we are all gone, they will come out and the tunnel between Lincoln
Center
and Columbus Circle will be alive all night.
This is their home; these meandering tunnels provide shelter from the cold reality
above.
The reality that will come beaming in upon them at the crack of dawn the next
morning,

when the Manhattan Line once again winds up her engines, as the sun rises on the Hudson River.

You can hear her coming around the bend, click-clack, click-clack,
as the shiny shopping cart clips along the tile until they both some into view.
All her belongings are on, in, or attached to her Main Line
as she pushes her way down the corridor, and through this life.
She rolls along amidst the puddles and the rubble left behind
from those who passed this way earlier today,
taking the Manhattan Line to and from their destinations.
The Lincoln Tunnel is her home for now, where she lays her head at night.
It reminders her of the hometown in the Midwest that she has not seen for years.
The Lincoln Center sign brings a calmness to her world and a peace within her heart.

She is rarely afraid or sad, as she has seen much worse than these abandoned by-ways have to offer. The rodents are the worst part, but even they seem to respect her, or at least acknowledge
the darkness within her that keeps them at bay.
She is not hopeless, just tired.
Worn out from all that she has experienced and seen in this life.
But mostly, tired of not being understood and respected.
Most days it's as if she is not even seen, that she has an invisibility about her,
that ironically, she has virtually no control over.

She wished she would have been able to wield that trait more when she was
deployed overseas in the military, or maybe she did and simply did not realize it.
Maybe she used her cloaking device at those critical moments when survival
was paramount and attack was imminent.
In any case, few rarely see her now as she makes her way along the tiled corridor.
The rolling wheels tap out a cadence all their own that repeats itself over and over.
It takes her back to basic training and the rhythmic calls the drill sergeant would
chant out, expecting all to repeat it back to him. She was mostly invisible then,
only speaking up when she needed to, or when she had to for survival
or to help one of the young girls that did not know what she was doing.

It's not much different now, as she speaks only when she needs to
and sometimes the words are conveyed simply through
a look or an act, and the message rings the same.

I see you.
I see you are cold. I see you are hurting.
I see you are in pain. I see you.
I see you have walked a long and weary road.
I see you have lost much.
I see you care. I see you
I see the light in you. I see your grit.
I see you want to be whole again. I see you.
Maybe no one else does. Maybe no one else sees.
Maybe no one else knows. But I do. I see you.
Click-clack, click-clack, here she comes.
Don't you hear her?
Don't you see her?
I do!

FLIGHT HOME

by Andy Gueck

It was another day in the bush, the heat, the bugs, the ever present fear that Charlie would ambush us. Just another day in the hell hole we called the Republic of South Vietnam. We had just completed a mission, done our job for God and Country or at least for Westmoreland, or at a minimum someone up the chain of command. We were headed in, looking for a chance to shower, have a beer, drink water that did not taste of chlorine and maybe, just maybe change into clean uniforms, and if we had been especially good, have a letter from home to read. The more time you spend in the bush, field, Indian country, whatever you care to call it, the smaller pleasures to make you happy become.

As we approached the fire base we were due to air lift from, our step became easier; the packs became lighter, and we could almost feel the wonderful feeling of a shower beating down upon us as we cleared the outlaying guards and approached the gate. Suddenly, we were inside and as we realized that someone else was now responsible for security, the weight of our mission began to fade away. Yes, we still had a debrief to attend to, but that was then, not now. Now was drop the packs, sit down, have a drink of water and a meal that was not reconstituted. Small pleasures. We could hear the sound of a chopper approaching, and knowing it was our ride to our base camp, we began to saddle up and prepare to board as soon as it landed to get further from the bush and closer to our current definition of civilization. Ours was not fancy, but we had beds, a modicum of privacy, showers, clean clothes, someone to stand guard, real food prepared in kitchens staffed by mess personnel.

The chopper landed, and as we settled either into our seats or onto the floor, we heard the most wonderful words in the world: "Gueck and Caldwell, you are going home; you got orders."

I just stared at the clerk, unable to believe that the end was at hand, that I was not going to be at war any more. As the words slowly sank in, I heard our team leader ask, "What about the rest of the team? We all arrived in country in the same week." The clerk replied with a shrug and indicated he knew nothing, typical poge.

The flight that probably took 30 minutes, seemed to last forever. Until I saw the orders, had them in my hand, started the out processing, I just knew it was a huge practical joke and the dream would burst as soon as we arrived at base camp.

I watched the ground rise up to meet the skids on the bird and felt the landing. The pilot began his shut down sequence, and the rotors began to slow as we moved off and away from the bird. Could this really be my last ride from Indian country? Was I really going home? Was my time in hell done! What about our team? Only two of us had orders, and as that question crossed my mind, our team leader announced that he would check on the orders and hand deliver them as well as check on the rest of the team.

We all headed to our quarters and the long anticipated showers. We had been in the field way too long.

Our uniforms were ripped, rotting, and not worth saving. As we left our quarters, mostly nude except for a modesty towel, all of us with our farmer tans, we moved almost in mass to the showers. Each of us grabbed a cold beer and downed most of it in a single gulp. The second beer lasted at least until the shower, and most of us sipped as we stood under the streams of water as the dirt, sweat, and whatever sluiced from our bodies and went down the drain and out of our lives in what we thought was forever. Man, were we wrong. Once each of us completed our shower time, teeth and other areas comfortably clean, we headed back to quarters to get clean clothes on and hopefully something to eat.

As we put on clean uniforms, dirty boots, and started thinking about more beer and food, the Commander walked in and hollered to everyone on his team, "Gather around. I have news and orders." We were there in almost an instant. Someone handed him a beer, and we waited, hoped, prayed and sweated, not knowing. We could see the huge three-inch stack of papers in his hand, knowing someone was leaving. We were all inching closer as not to miss a word.

"First, Gueck and Coleman, I have your orders. Jones, yours are here as well. Congrats, men. You survived and are going home. I will talk to each of you later. Everyone else, the word is orders will be coming down and will be ready ASAP. Best news is, no more patrols as we are so shorthanded now and so few days left in-country."

As I was handed my ticket to a plane ride back to the World, I could only stand there and stare, first at the paper that said I was going home, then at my friends, those with the paper and those without. Not knowing what to say or do, I just walked up to each of them and hugged the people who had saved my life and whose lives I cherished as much if not more than my own.

Suddenly, Jones hollered, "I got dibs on the jeep to out-process, anyone going with me?" As the three of us piled into the jeep, we headed toward the administration building to get our out-processing sheet and get started. When I started to read my orders, I realized we could actually leave Phu Bai that evening to Da Nang and then to Saigon the next day.

When we stormed into the admin building, you need to understand that field troops—us, and garrison troops—the admin people do not always get along. As field troops, we are used to be in control or at least with an option; whereas, the garrison troops have a daily routine that they do not like to have disturbed or disrupted. Three raggedy, though clean field troops charging into their domain is not part of their schedule and seeing weapons on each of us, further disrupted their world.

We lined up to request our paperwork, but it was obvious that rapid responses were not on the first order of their agenda. A young officer looked up from his desk as we boisterously intruded into his quiet, orderly world. He stood up and in a voice that strove to be a command tone asked, "What are you doing in this office under arms?"

The response was simple, "We are under orders and need our out-processing paperwork."

The now worried looking young officer almost shouted to us to get out his office and never come back. Fortunately, a senior officer, the S-1, Administrative Officer, stepped out of his office at the shouting of his subordinate, took a quick look at the situation, and turned to his Sargent Major and told the Top to take care of us. He then requested that the young officer join him in his office. The Sargent Major approached the counter, and without a word, handed each of us on out processing form. With a look that seemed wistful, he quietly offered us a "Congrats and have a safe trip home, gentlemen."

With a hurried, "Thanks, Top," we grabbed our paper and departed the area. With that piece of paper in hand, we now knew where we needed to go and to some extent the order. We rushed off to the finance office which was on a distant part of the post and not easily accessible from our compound. When we arrived, we were requested to leave all weapons outside unless we were payroll guards. We flipped a coin and Jones lost. We left our rifles with him and the two of us headed inside to clear finance. I had taken Jones' paperwork with me just in case. We approached the counter and asked what we needed to do to out-process. Fortunately, we found that all that was needed was a check to see if we had any payroll on the books and receive an initial on our forms.

Our next stop was to the company headquarters so we could clear and get ready to leave for Da Nang. We pulled up in front of the HQ and barged into the office. At that same moment, the Commander and our team commander were exiting the office. Our team leader just looked at us and shook his head, and told us that before we could out-process, debriefs were due. We just stared at him, and the air became so tense that it was almost visible. The two Commanders then smiled and said, "Kidding. Get your stuff turned in, make supply happy, and come back here and we will get you cleared."

Clearing supply was almost too easy. We all had worn through so many uniforms that we were wearing almost rags. We requested new uniforms and boots, so we at least did not tear our clothes. We were issued two sets of new uniforms. We stopped right there and changed in the supply room. Modesty was not an issue, but clean clothes were. Boots were placed carefully to the side because it would take a day or two to break them in.

The last items to be turned in were our weapons. We were going to have to spend our last few hours in Vietnam without the security of our weapons. Weapons we had carried for a year, all day every day. Weapons that saved our lives, that were part of ourselves beyond understanding. We looked at each other and called our Commander to see if we could turn our weapons in when we got to Saigon. The immediate answer was not only NO, but a loud and obscene NO. Now, feeling naked to the world, we cleared supply and headed back to the company headquarters to finish our out processing and get a flight to Da Nang.

Goodbyes were short, quick, and almost nonexistent. We were relived of our jeep and given a ride to the chopper pad. Again, a quick good luck and so long, and there we were: duffel bag, newer fatigues, and no weapons. About as we arrived in country. Fortunately, a flight of choppers arrived within an hour and when asked, rides were quickly given to take us to Da Nang.

When the birds lifted off, it really hit me. We were leaving this shit hole and headed back to the world. I sat in the chopper seat, my head hanging down to hide my emotions and just relished that I was going home. After a 45-minute flight, we landed at the chopper pad at Da Nang. The chopper crews wished us good luck and there we were. We headed to the nearest Orderly Room and asked to see the First Sargent. When we told to enter, we walked in and politely asked if a ride was available to finance. Then we went to transit quarters so we could clear and head to Saigon the next morning. Fortunately, Top was in a good mood and hollered for his driver, giving him instructions to get us cleared through finance, fed, and bedded down next to the airport. We were told that the first normal flight headed south was an 8 a.m. takeoff. We would need to be at the terminal by 7.

After thanking Top, we jumped into his jeep to go to Finance where we were issued our "travel pay". In each case, travel was via aircraft, coach to our next duty station or our home. The Army way, all in cash, 20 dollar bills. Way too much cash, but away we went. We got to the open mess (dinner) just before it closed and were well fed. Then to the transit billets for a place to sleep. I am sure that we did sleep, but I know I spent way too many sleep minutes thinking, "I am going home, home, no more jungle."

The next morning, we were all up and dressed by six. To the open mess for coffee and then the short walk to the airfield. One thing we did not turn in was our in-country travel orders. They gave us a priority for boarding and we did use them that morning. By noon we were in Saigon at the out processing center known as Camp Alpha.

Camp Alpha could be qualified as a very busy military motel. Most Army personnel were processed via Alpha, so there were barracks, single and double rooms, a restaurant, and a bar. We reported in to Alpha as out-processing and were assigned beds and given a roster of the out-processing tasks to complete. The only major one was urinalysis. Just before departure at the airfield, we would be subject to a customs' inspection. As it was still early, we asked if we could visit the pee center now and hurry our departure time and date. We were informed that we were scheduled for pee duty at 9 a.m. the next morning and for a 3p.m. departure in the afternoon. Suddenly, it all became real; we really were going home.

We headed to our quarters. As we were NCO's, we had a four bed room. A place to secure our gear and perhaps sleep. We headed to the Open Mess and the bar to find a way to pass the afternoon and evening until we were rostered to fill the cup. We found a table and realized that there was nothing to do at Alpha but drink or drink. We were sitting, talking about nothing when I looked up and there was someone from my language school class. He came over, and after introducing him to my teammates, we caught up on other classmates. As the evening progressed, we all caught up with friends we had not seen in a year or more. Proof of the statement, "Small world." Or, to remember a classic movie line, "Of all the gin joints in the world, why in this one?"

Sometime during the night, we all struggled back to our quarters and crashed. At 7 a.m., we were rousted out for breakfast and prepped for the pee exercise. As I stood behind my blue line, cup in hand, I was grateful that the US Army was searching for drug use, not booze abuse. We all passed.

Upon arrival back at our quarters, we were told to police up our gear and prepare to muster for DEROS (Date Expected Return Over Seas) flight. I stopped and looked at a calendar, realizing that I have been in Viet Nam for 364 days. By the time I returned to California, I would have been gone an entire year.

We were bused to the airfield, Ton Son Nhut, the same place we arrived. It looked the same. The only differences were that I could not smell Nam any more, and I had no fear as to what would happen. Suddenly, we were marched to the tarmac, and we stood near a plane as it began to deplane a new levee of soldiers—fresh meat. Looking back I am sure I looked just like the soldiers I saw when I arrived in country.

They needed to prep the aircraft, but for some reason, we were not rushing anyone. We knew this was our craft, our ride home, and we could wait. We only had to wait a few minutes as they were refueling in Japan, and suddenly we were invited on, a quick roster check, and…aircraft seats that were not just straps, stewardesses with smiling faces welcoming us on the aircraft. Everything a reminder that we were headed home. A welcome from the crew, safety briefing, and the door closed; the aircraft was moving. Each of us in our own way were helping the craft take off. A huge cheer, we are safe, out of Viet Nam and going home.

The flight home was the exact opposite of the route to the Nam, Japan, Alaska, and last but not least, Travis AFB, USA. As we landed and deplaned, we endured another customs inspection but it was of no major effort. Then we were offered rides to either San Francisco International Airport or to Oakland Army

Replacement Depot for new uniforms, a steak dinner, and then transport to the mode of our travel to our next destination. Several of us opted to go directly to the airport so we could get early flights east. I was headed to Chicago and suspected I could fly out fairly early. We arrived at the airport mid evening. Still light out, we could see the skyline of San Francisco, and yes, the view was beautiful. However, I have never returned to California since my plane lifted off and headed east.

As we arrived at the terminal, we remembered the stories of other returnees about how the reception was due to the huge anti-war sentiment, and we only wanted to get something to eat, a place to sit and unwind and mentally prepare to re-enter a world that we were not prepared to join. We knew that sirens, loud noises, shouts, and multiple other sounds were not an indicator of someone trying to do us harm. We knew that kicking open a door, throwing a grenade through the opening and following with gunfire to announce our arrival was not going to be accepted by the polite society we hoped to reenter.

Unfortunately, as we headed from the ticket counter to the departure area where we planned to eat and drink until our various flights were called, we began to walk through a gauntlet of some civilians. Now, I admit, one of the individuals standing there was the vision of the California Girl, long bleached blond hair, blue eyes, tight jeans, and a very thin tee shirt, lovely bumps protruding from the upper part of the shirt: the very vision of part of who and what we had in our minds and fought for over there.

As we approached these individuals, the one officer with us spoke quietly, "Keep it together." The hippies began to harass us verbally with anti-war slogans and chants, but that was like rain, rolling off, but the vision of American woman-hood whom we all had admired as we approached felt it was acceptable for her to spit on us or at least on our uniforms. We recoiled but did not respond as would have been normal. Other travelers walked on by as if nothing was happening.

That was our introduction to how we could expect to be treated by the country we fought to defend.

THE HEALING WALL

by Andy Gueck

The Wall, the Dark Obelisk, a place of names.
We have all heard of the Wall, the Healing Wall.
But who is it expected to heal?
The soldier approaches the Wall to find closure,
To say good-bye, to say I'm sorry.
There is no healing.

The family who searches the Wall to find a name,
to put closure to the hole torn within their hearts.
Every parent hopes that the telegram was wrong,
That the name they seek is not there.
As they reach the year, the day, the line,
they find the name they so hoped was not there.
Tears stream down her cheeks, weathered with age and sorrow,
his eyes lose some of their luster in knowing the truth.
The child seeking someone who was never there,
touches a name, takes a shading, but receives no answers.

Is this healing?
There is no healing.
But wait, there were those who protested
who stood and chanted, hoped to change the world
but in change came hatred not of the cause, but of the enactors.

Those who hated the soldier.
The soldier who had been a school mate.
The soldier who was drafted and sent to war.
The soldier who watched his friends die.
The soldier who feared for his life and limb.
The soldier who slept with his rifle as his lover.

Why do you hate him?
Because he was brave, unlucky, alive, stronger, wiser?
Or because he did what you did not and as you see him
you see what you are not?

The Healing Wall is not for the soldier.
It is for the person who spit on soldiers.
The person who called soldiers "baby killers."
The person who put down soldiers as worthless.
These people need to heal, to learn to forgive themselves.
The soldier cannot heal them.
The soldier will not heal them.

WARRIOR WRITERS'
CONTRIBUTOR BIOGRAPHIES

John Achor's writing assignments have appeared in a variety of local, national and international publications. He enjoys writing about, "The subjects I know best: the military, flying and people I've known." After that, John says he lets a vivid imagination take over.

In the tradition of military life, he and his wife moved to Arkansas in 1999, and now reside in Nebraska. John has been a professional writer since the 1990s.

John's third novel in the Casey Fremont mystery series (Five, Six - Deadly Mix) featuring his lady amateur sleuth, was released early in 2018, and will be followed by a pair of thrillers featuring Alex Hilliard, a USAF officer. The fourth Casey mystery is growing on his computer.

Mary Baker, US Air Force/Nebraska Air Guard; Master Sergeant Retired

Mary has been a writer and communicator her entire life. English and creative writing classes were always her favorite subjects in school, where she was the editor of her high school newspaper, the Waverly Hi-Spot, during her senior year. An Air Force veteran, Mary retired from the 155th Air Refueling Wing, Nebraska Air National Guard in February of 2013, after 24 years of service to her country. During her military career she held jobs as an image processor and interpreter for the reconnaissance mission; she worked in the finance office processing travel and pay vouchers; was a section supervisor for the 155th Force Support Squadron; for seven years she flew all over the world as an inflight refueling specialist, or a *boomer;* and she served as the first sergeant to the 155th Mission Support Group Commander and Airmen. Throughout Mary's professional life and career, she has written numerous professional documents, pieces for newsletters and many other writings for her job requirements. Mary has been with the Warrior Writer Group since its inception in the fall of 2014. As one of the three original veterans from that inaugural group still attending the writing sessions today, Mary continues to be inspired by her peers and encouraged in her writing pursuits by both the facilitators and her fellow veteran writers. Mary's writing goals for the next five-years include: to write more and work less; to publish several stories/pieces; to put her song lyrics to music; to read her writings in public forums; and to outline and compose a couple of her book ideas. The Warrior Writer groups are a top priority for Mary, and she always looks forward to the next session to write with her extended family.

Jennifer Barrett grew up in Papillion, NE and considers herself a true Midwesterner at heart, despite life and travels taking her away from the Great Plains, at various times. A veteran of the United States Air Force, she spent most of her time in the service as a weather officer in Germany. Barrett holds a Bachelor of Science in Meteorology from the University of Nebraska and a master's degree in Theological Studies in Marriage and Family from the John Paul II Institute in Washington D.C. When not writing, she spends her time raising four wonderful children, and enjoying the loving and unending support of her Active Duty Air Force husband.

Raymond Bates

I am a Vietnam Vet, who was a Navy Corpsman, attached to a Marine line unit in I Corp, RVN. After six months in the bush, I was transferred to Dong Ha Battalion Aid station. I was transferred to Battalion Aid at Phu Bai, and then back to Dong Ha. These transfers were due to the need of corpsmen needed for Tet of 68. During my tour I earned six Battle Stars.

This writers' group has been wonderful for me in that it has helped me open up those areas closed for my well-being in the past. I had buried those memories and now, being around other Vets and writers, this journey to healing is eased.

Jim Carlton was born and grew up on the U.S. West Coast in Fresno, California. After graduating from high school, he served in the United States Navy onboard the attack aircraft carrier USS Ticonderoga (CVA-14), which did duty off the coast of Vietnam in 1965-66. Following his military service, Jim returned home to Fresno and attended college at California State University Fresno obtaining a Bachelor of Arts Degree in journalism. Following college, he had a 40-year career in journalism, which included stints as a newspaper reporter for several newspapers in the Pacific Northwest and Nebraska, editor of agricultural-related magazines, and as a freelance writer. He has resided in Lincoln, Nebraska on and off since 1984.

John F. Costello graduated from Cathedral High Omaha in '64 and Seminary/priesthood study with Benedictines. He received his BA in '71 and MS in '76. His military service includes one year US Navy in-country with NSA Da Nang, Vietnam. USCG Reserve-retired 21 years Port Security foreign vessel inspector and boating safety. VA Medical Center, Retired, Vocational Rehab and HR Specialist, LA, Chicago and Wilkes Barre.

"Employer of the Year" award recipient in 2006 and 1996 by California governor. Placed hundreds of job seekers in over 30 federal agencies. Coordinated 9 federal job fairs attended by over 50 federal agencies, over 10 thousand job seekers, covered by major network news media. Testified before U.S. Congress, Banking & Finance committee regarding LA job market as HR Specialist. Community Service Award by LA City Council in 1998. Knight of the year in 2000 by Knights of Columbus, Van Nuys, CA. Co-founder-director of www.lamarchforlife with Knights of Columbus from 2003-20014.

Successfully generated over "$90,000 in fund raising for Knights of Columbus—Sanctity of Life, 2 local orphanages and VA Tennis Clubs, boosting employee morale through athletic competition. Started and directed tennis clubs at UNMC—Omaha, and VA hospitals in LA and Pennsylvania. Press Agent and fundraiser for Magda Brown, Holocaust –Survivor-Speaker in Chicago.

Cindy Cronn is a retired art teacher who has always enjoyed writing. She became involved with the Nebraska Writing Project when her school district supported an embedded writing workshop during which she joined other teachers in an effort to provide writing opportunities for students in all academic areas. She enjoys writing essays and poetry and is inspired by the writers and presenters in the Omaha Warrior Writers group that she helps facilitate.

Steven DeLair was born in Wyoming and raised mostly in Nebraska. He received his BFA from the University of Nebraska in 1967 and subsequently joined the

Marines. He served as an Infantry Platoon Commander and Civil Affairs Officer in South Vietnam in 1968 and 1969.

In 1970 he joined a large insurance company in California and later Arizona. In 1981 he left the insurance business and began his career as an artist. In 1996 Steven returned to Lincoln where he continues his career as an artist.

The American Dream paper was presented to the Lincoln Torch Club in 2014.

Donald Dingman is a retired engineering draftsman. With a national certification in fire alarm systems, he has assisted engineers in laying out fire alarm systems all over the country, including the Pinnacle Bank Arena in Lincoln. He also served on a City of Lincoln's Fire Code Board for almost 30 years.

Dingman served in the Navy at Naval Air Station in Brunswick, Maine and aboard the U.S.S. Tripoli, LPH-10, off Vietnam and in the Indian Ocean. He was a parachute rigger, achieving the rank of PR2 in under three years. His work helped the ship's aircrew rescue six pilots from shark infested waters. He also began skydiving during this time, jumping in the U.S. Philippines and Singapore. Dingman held a USPA Instructor rating. His article on jumping with a flag was published in the *Parachutist* magazine.

Dingman enjoys writing romantic fiction with eight un-published novels and numerous short stories to date. When he isn't writing, he is on his bicycle riding the trails of Lincoln, or working as a volunteer camera operator for the Brown Bag lectures at the Nebraska History Museum. He is married and lives in Lincoln. They have one son who is living in Bozeman, Montana.

Cynthia Douglas-Ybarra is an Army veteran who also happens to be a writer. She is also an RN for the Department of Veterans' Affairs working as a Clinical Documentation Improvement Analyst. She enjoys the camaraderie and professionalism of Warrior Writers and encourages any Veteran to come and join. Warrior Writers has provided her a safe place to share her narrative nonfiction, prose, and poetry.

Joel Elwell was born and raised in Lincoln, NE. He is a Marine Corps veteran, extremely patriotic, and is an active participant in the Warrior Writer's group at the Lincoln VA. His interests include (but are not limited to!): spending time with his family, their slobbery Great Pyrenees and their odd cat, reading, writing, hunting, fishing, golfing and playing a pretty mean game of pool. He also considers himself the world's biggest Stephen King fan, although Mr. King has yet to confirm this.

Andy Gueck is a Vietnam veteran. He began writing when the opportunity arose to join a group of other veterans and family in a free writing group sponsored at the local VA. In the beginning, he felt he was very rough and totally unpolished. His work was not precise nor was it public worthy. However, as he had been a storyteller for many years, he learned to condense his writing, expand the descriptions and offer work that can touch many. He is a very proud member of the first group of Warrior Writers in Nebraska.

Beverly Hoistad is an avid reader, researcher for the writing years ahead. A seasoned teacher/coordinator in Houston ISD (10) and Lincoln Public Schools (26), she's taught writing to various ages (6-76) during and after school, nights, and weekends, for over 36 years and Nebraska Writing Project and other classes at the graduate level at the the University of Nebraska, too. She's edited and critiqued books, written curriculum for a national series at PBS and for second grade writing for Lincoln Public Schools, adopted by the Special Education Services at LPS. A Teacher Consultant/Coordinator for the Lincoln Warrior Writers, veterans still congregate, hazelnut coffee in one hand, multiple copies of a type-written story in the other, at the VA auditorium at 9 a.m. on Saturday mornings. She's learned a lot from them and still drops by occasionally. Best moments? The deep breath before "Author's Notes" and treating the "baby" gently!

Sara Hollcroft is a life-long learner with a BA in English, speech and drama and a minor in journalism and a MA in English. Her teaching experience includes Palmyra High School, Lincoln Public Schools, Southeast Community College in Lincoln, and Wesleyan University. She was one of five who trained as an EMT and founded the Palmyra Rescue Squad, serving as its first president. She is on the Nebraska Writing Project board and co-leads the Lincoln area Warrior Writers. Her father, husband, and daughter all served their country via the army and navy. She lives with her husband in Lincoln, Nebraska, where she spends her free time reading and writing.

Dean E. Hyde grew up in North Platte, Nebraska, graduating from high school in 1963. In 1968 he graduated from University of Nebraska. He was drafted and sent to Fort Lewis Washington for Basic Training, then to a Signal Corp School at Fort Gordon, GA., then onto Long Binh, Vietnam arriving on his birthday March 4, 1969.

Hyde served as a Communication Center Specialist at the American Division Headquarters in southern I Corp. At Chu Lai, Hyde received a Direct Commission as a 2nd Lieutenant. Next, he was transferred to Saigon to work in a Communication Center in MACV headquarters. Returning to United States, he was assigned to the International Logistics Center, New Cumberland Army Depot in Pennsylvania then to Fort Gordon in GA. Hyde left active duty in 1978 but continued his military service in an Individual Mobilization Reserve program. After nine and a half years of active duty and 17 years in the Army Reserves, Hyde retired as a Lieutenant Colonel in May of 1995.

Hyde has written on a wide variety of topics with the NE Warrior Writers. Since his participation in this group, he has published one novel, *Flight Risk,* which is available on Amazon.

Mandy Kottas is an Air National Guard veteran who served from 2014-2017. She graduated from the university of Nebraska-Lincoln with her Masters in Architecture in 2012. She focuses her writing on helping and teaching others, usually through nonfiction. Today, she focuses her creative energy on art and literature. "Under the Desk" was inspired by her college writings about visual prompts combined with her recent nonfiction writings about her military.

Guadalupe J. Mier was born in Waelder, Texas on December 12, 1943. Raised and schooled in Houston (TX), he attended the local University of St Thomas where he wrote short stories for their Shadwell Sampler. In January 1968, he received his Master's in Library Science at Louisiana State University followed by full-time employment at Houston Public Library. In June 1968, Uncle Sam drafted him.

The Army trained him as an Operating Room Technician, but on arrival in October 1969 at Camp Enari near Pleiku, Vietnam, he was assigned regular Medic duties: patrols in the "boonies" and convoy duty with the Military Police through Pleiku to Kontum, Dak To and Ben Het. When on base, he worked in the operating room (mainly septic procedures) and was fortunate to assist in the birth of an American-Vietnamese child! Between work and recreation, he wrote poems about his adventures as a medic. The last 6 months of his tour he was assigned Camp

Radcliff at An Khe mostly on the midnight shift at 4th Med Clearing Station, with lots of time to write. This fun tour ended October 1970 and he was assigned to Ft Carson, Colorado where he completed active duty on 7/29/71.

Returning to Houston Public Library in December 1971 (thanks to a city policy that granted military leave) he worked in various positions including a 3-year project with 4 other major U.S. libraries, and also two stints as a branch librarian. He moved down the Texas coast and up the library ladder thereafter. In June, 1989 he became Director at Bellevue (NE) Public Library and retired after 25 years in December 2014. For 6 months following, he served as Interim Director at Omaha Public Library. He opened their monthly department meetings with a poem (not his).

John Petelle is a Desert Storm veteran of the Marine Corps. His previous careers includes time as an editor, elementary school instructor, and veteran's service officer. He writes full-time, primarily in the genres of fantasy, science-fiction and poetry.

Current and publication credits include Ghost City Press, Pedestal Magazine, A Fifth of Boo! Anthology Vol. 5, Speculative City and the ConStellation X Poetry Contest.

Artistic inspirations include Anne McCaffery, Glen Cook, Anne Lamott and Julia Cameron.

John lives in Lincoln, Nebraska with a family that includes his wife and multiple furred and finned creatures.

Jack Rainier Pryor is a writer based in the Omaha metro area of Nebraska. He writes memoir, essay, short stories, and poetry. He is an Air Force veteran.

CW2 **Robrenana Redl**, ARNG, Retired, went from Army brat to Army veteran. Most of her military career was spent in human resources and family programs, also fulfilling the role of an Equal Opportunity Advisor. She has a Bachelor's degree in Business Management through Bellevue University. Aside from the military sector, Redl has worked in the business, education, and non-profit sectors. She currently works for *I've Got a Name,* an anti-sex trafficking, non-profit organization in Nebraska. Redl is a Trauma Healing Facilitator through the American Bible Society and the founder and host of the podcast *G.R.I.T Getting Real: Immersed in Truth.* She is currently working on a young adult fiction book.

Redl lives in Lincoln, Nebraska with her husband, Troy, also retired military, her two young adult children, and their 60-pound dog, Evie.

Sharon Robino-West's passion is serving the underserved or what she calls "special populations" through her love of writing and photography. She has been a member of Nebraska Warrior Writers since its inception in 2014 as well as a member of the Writers Guild initiative in NYC since 2011. She has published a short story called, "I Honor You", regarding her son's service in Iraq and has had several pieces read from the stage in NYC, including one read by Alfre Woodward in 2015. She is currently working on a memoir. She also leads healing writing group using the AWA method.

Tom Seib has served as a teacher and administrator for 46 years in private schools in Nebraska. He has served as a facilitator for the Nebraska Warrior Writers program since 2016 in Lincoln. Seib has also taught and led numerous Holocaust educator consortiums and workshops across the country since 2008 and is a member of the Nebraska Writing Project. He enjoys writing poetry and short stories centering on rural life in the Midwest.

William L. (Bill) Smutko served in the U.S. Army. He enlisted in January 1967 and was released from active duty as a Captain in June 1973. He was stationed with the 9th Infantry Division in Vietnam from November 1968 through November 1970.

He has a bachelor's degree in English from Western State Colorado University, Gunnison, Colorado, and a master's in Business Administration from the University of Nebraska - Lincoln.

He spent six seasons as a guide and outfitter in Saskatchewan and Montana.

He planted a vineyard in 1999 and raised wine grapes until they sold the vineyard in 2018.

He has had five short stories published: "Death of a Warrior" in *The Deadly Writers Patrol,* "Last Man Fallen" online by the Veterans' Writing Project, "Fidget" in the 2018 Nebraska Writers' Guild anthology *Voices From the Plains,* and "Ichetucknee, and The Raft" in the 2019 *Voices from The Plains.*

Fred Snowardt was born and raised in O'Neill, Nebraska, graduating St. Mary's Academy and then joined the Navy, serving 4 years. He also served 16 years in the U.S. Air Force, returning to O'Neill where he operated a plumbing-heating air conditioning and refrigeration business. He graduated with honors after two years at UNK. He worked in the state probation system prior to retiring. He is a father of 4, grandfather of 8 and great-grandfather of 12.

Jen Stastny gratefully co-facilitates the Nebraska Warrior Writers in Omaha. She has been a teacher at Omaha Central High School since 1998 and first participated in the Nebraska Writing Project nearly two decades ago. She earned B.A.'s in English and French as well as her teaching certification in Secondary Language Arts and Secondary Modern Languages at UNL and her M.A. in Literature at UNO. She believes in the power of the written word to create community and improve our lives.

CPSIA information can be obtained
at www.ICGtesting.com
Printed in the USA
LVHW090214201120
672241LV00005B/52